LAKE ZURICH MIDDLE SCHOOL
NORTH CAMPUS
LAKE ZURICH, ILLINOIS 60047

A Place to Hide

ALSO BY ROBERT WESTALL:

In Camera and Other Stories

Yaxley's Cat

The Promise

Blitzcat

Ghost Abbey

A PLACE TO HIDE

ROBERT WESTALL

LAKE ZURICH MIDDLE SCHOOL
NORTH CAMPUS
LAKE ZURICH, ILLINOIS 60047

**SCHOLASTIC
HARDCOVER**

Scholastic Inc.
New York

Copyright © 1994 by Robert Westall.
All rights reserved. Published by Scholastic Inc.,
555 Broadway, New York, NY 10012,
by arrangement with Pan Macmillan Children's Books, London.
SCHOLASTIC HARDCOVER is a registered trademark of Scholastic Inc.

No part of this publication may be reproduced in whole or in part, or stored in a retrieval
system, or transmitted in any form or by any means, electronic, mechanical, photocopying, recording, or otherwise, without written permission of the publisher. For
information regarding permission, write to Scholastic Inc., 555 Broadway, New York,
NY 10012.

Library of Congress Cataloging-in-Publication Data

Westall, Robert.
   A place to hide / Robert Westall.
      p.   cm.
   Summary: When the British government decides to have her father killed for
exposing political corruption, eighteen-year-old Lucy is forced to leave her home and
establish a new identity.

ISBN 0-590-47748-X

[1. Fathers and daughters — Fiction.   2. Identity — Fiction.   3. Whistle blow-
ing — Fiction.   4. Political corruption — Fiction.   5. England — Fiction.]   I. Title.
PZ7.W51953P1   1994
[Fic]—dc20   93-34592
                                                                                    CIP
                                                                                     AC

12 11 10 9 8 7 6 5 4 3 2 1   4 5 6 7 8 9/9

Printed in the U.S.A.   37

First Scholastic printing, October 1994

For Clarissa Cridland
Thanks for all the tales and sales

Chapter One

It was her last half-happy day. The last day she felt safe.

She laboured joyfully. June sun poured in through the exam-room window, making a bar of burning gold across her desk. Sweat trickled down her spine, and made her hand stick to the paper.

But she was on the last question and knew the answer. Ideas rolled through her mind like triumphant waves. Even though her writing-hand felt like somebody had driven a nail through it. She wanted to stop and flex it, but there were only five minutes to go, and the great rolling ideas wouldn't let her.

'Stop!' cried Mr Betts. But her hand raced on like a car out of control. Until he cried 'stop' a second time.

Sighs and groans and stretching from the ranked desks, that nothing could stop. Not even Mr Betts saying sharply, 'No talking.' Then the fuss with little bits of string.

When Mr Betts took her paper, he grinned. She knew he'd been watching her, all through the exam. He caught her up, on the front steps of the hall, afterwards.

'That seemed to go all right . . . ?'

'That one was OK. But the first paper . . .'

'I heard you did OK on that one too.'

Which meant he'd gone to the school office to have a sneak read, while they were doing the papers up. Teachers did that. With their favourites.

Why was she Bettsy's favourite? Ever since she'd been a

1

scared little thing in the first year and he'd been a terrifying giant with a flaming red beard. When you were scared of everything, why did you suddenly adore the most scary thing of all? The giant who flung exercise books right aross the room, so they fluttered their pages like terrified hens. The giant who bellowed rude comments to accompany the flight of books.

'Waste of paper and ink, Monks!'

'Brilliant, Smurthwaite! Five pages and not a single thought!'

But when he'd flung hers, he'd shouted:

'A miracle! A girl who thinks for herself!'

Mind you, the book had hit her on the nose, bringing tears to her eyes. But when she'd blinked back the tears, she saw he'd given her nine out of ten.

He never gave ten. But she had slaved over the years to always get nine. Once she'd only got seven, and he'd said nothing, just handed her the book back, tight-lipped, so she could've cried.

Bettsy had always taught her history class. Except for the third year, with wimp Marsden, which had been a dreary desert without Bettsy banging on his desk and impersonating Napoleon at Waterloo with his execrable French accent. Or telling them things he got up to as a kid and throwing back his head and laughing, showing all his gold fillings. Bettsy with his ever-lasting old sportscoat, patched at the elbow, and the pipe he smoked while riding his bike, and his breath that always smelt comfortingly of tobacco.

How had she always managed to keep Bettsy? Or was it Bettsy who had kept *her*? He arranged the timetable . . . Sometimes she wondered which, tucked up safe in bed at night; but even in bed this thought was barely thinkable, and made her wriggle her toes with confusion.

She came back to the present.

2

And at that moment, the first awful thing happened. She looked at him, standing on the hall steps, and realized with a shock that seven years had changed him. Where once he had seemed a giant, he was little taller than she was now. Why had his schoolmaster's stoop got suddenly worse? There were white hairs, amongst the redness of his beard. And so many lines on his face. Not just the fierce deep lines on his forehead (for he had always been a monstrous frowner) but weak wavering lines on his cheeks, too, like you might find on a shrivelling apple.

A cold hand squeezed her heart. Bettsy was not some immortal god. One day soon he would be old and grey. One day he would die. The wrongness of it was terrible. People like Bettsy should always be there to come back to . . .

'Well, not to worry,' said Bettsy. 'Nothing you can do about the exams now. Go and enjoy yourself. Play tennis. Lie in the sun.'

He held out his hand. She realized it was a final goodbye. She took his hand for the first time ever; warm, firm, crinkly like an old leather glove.

'Drop me a line from Cambridge. And look us up at the end of term.'

'I will.' People did. But it never worked. She'd watched it happen so often. Hello, how are you? Big smiles, big handshakes. How's X? Have you seen Y? Then awkwardness; silences growing. Another handshake. Call any time. Goodbye.

No more Bettsy every day, sure as tap-water. But what could you do about it? Nothing, except say, 'Thanks for everything.' Thanks for believing in me, when I didn't believe in myself.

'No thanks required,' said Bettsy. 'It's what they pay us for.'

Though she knew he was pleased. Then he added, with a

3

grin that made him look young again, 'Glad you approve of us. Plenty don't.'

But he was still gently pushing her away. Like a parent blackbird pushing its young out of the nest, to fend for themselves. As he must have pushed so many away, over the years. To make room in his heart for those who would come.

She was nothing special. He must have his favourites in every year. She was part of a great crowd now. Of those who had loved and lost Bettsy.

He seemed to sense her desolation; to be dredging some word up for her alone. Finally, he squinted up at the sun and said softly, 'Don't let the powers-that-be con you, girl. Tutors, vice-chancellors . . . they all have to go for a pee, like everyone else. Even the Prime Minister, even the Queen, God bless her.'

Then, with a flick of his hand, he turned and went back into the hall. She noticed that he limped a little; his left leg. She wanted to run after him, to ask him what was wrong with it.

But she didn't. She emptied her locker in the prefects' room. Walked round the school for the last time. The exam had run late; it was gone five. The sun was still hot, but the sunlight was silent, haunted only by the screaming of swifts overhead, and the flitting of house-martins to their little nests of clay under the eaves. All summer the swifts would scream and the house-martins flit in the silent yard. Until the new term came, when she'd be forgotten.

As she was walking out of the gates, she saw a carefree third-year cycling wildly round the tennis courts. Cycling in the yard was forbidden. But she didn't stop him. She wasn't a prefect any more. She just envied him his four more happy years . . .

As if to mark the moment with a deadly magic, the sun

darkened. A coldness crept across her skin. Looking up, she saw massive clouds building up from the west.

After the endless sun of May and June, it seemed an omen.

It was.

Chapter Two

The darkness seemed to stay with Lucy; inside her head and out. The yellow-lit darkness of the Tube, full of swaying bodies. The darkness inside the house, as she knocked off the burglar alarm.

From force of habit she switched on Wimbledon and flopped down on the sofa. But it was a lousy one-sided match. Steffi Graf versus some poor unseeded rabbit. Who wasn't even making a fight of it. The rabbit kept serving double-faults, which made Lucy's heart sag in sympathy. Anything the rabbit did get over the net, Steffi swept back for a winner. Like swatting a fly. Why did unseeded rabbits offer themselves for such ritual humiliation?

It was as she sat there, too dispirited even to switch the farce off, that the smell of Mummy's room came to her.

The graveyard smell of year-old Chanel No. 5 mixed with dust.

Somebody had left the door of Mummy's room open *again*. It had been closed when she went to school this morning, she was sure. It was *always* kept shut. Ever since Mummy was killed. Daddy had insisted on it. Mrs Meggit, the cleaning lady, had had it drummed into her. Keeping that door shut was the only thing that made living in the house bearable.

But this week it had been left open twice. At first she'd thought it might be burglars. Except the burglar alarm was still on, and nothing was missing or even moved.

She'd wondered with a shiver about ghosts . . . but that was stupid.

It could only be Daddy, sneaking home in the afternoons from the Department while she was still at school.

But why?

She hadn't dared to ask. Her own pain about Mummy was too big; she had no wish to dig into Daddy's. Daddy had gone away inside himself when Mummy died, and never really come out again. Work, work, work, he brought a bulging briefcase home every night. They would eat their supper together, desperately trying to think of things to say, to fend off the silence that endlessly seeped from Mummy's empty place at table.

Then he was into his study, working, working, till she looked in with his supper-drink at eleven, to say goodnight.

Often he would not come upstairs till one or two, and then knock himself unconscious with sleeping pills.

And she seldom slept, till she heard his slippered foot on the stair.

And in the mornings, she would find his supper-drink on his desk, still undrunk, stone-cold. And imagine what things he must feel, in his hours alone . . .

Only on Sundays did he make an effort. After church they played tennis at the club, then relaxed over cool drinks. Then, after a late lunch, to an antiques fair in some country town, just as they had when Mummy was alive. Then telly together, until bed. She knew he had vowed to himself to give her Sundays. And he always kept his vows, whatever it cost.

Sometimes he would laugh on the tennis court, when the ball did something funny. But it wasn't a real laugh; more an impersonation of the laugh he'd laughed in happier times, as if he was trying to relearn the trick of it. Sometimes when he found a good piece of Staffordshire at an antiques fair, his face would light up, and he would haggle like a fiend. And be really alive while the haggling lasted. He might even stay alive all Sunday evening, the new piece of Staffordshire carefully placed under the reading lamp at his elbow, where he could glance and gloat over it.

But by the following day he would have lost interest . . .

And he wasn't getting any better; he was getting worse. He was moving further away from her all the time. Life at home was like lying in the bath too long, with the water getting cold and then really freezing, and you couldn't summon up the energy to get out.

That was how she was feeling now. God, she must do *something*. Or she'd just stop existing altogether. She leapt to her feet in a panic and went to ring Claire to arrange to play tennis tomorrow.

They had a good moan about tennis-playing rabbits, which made her feel part of the human race again. They discussed what to wear for the end-of-term party at Snowberry's and what a foul dump Snowberry's was, but the boys organized it . . .

But in the background she could hear Claire's young brothers shouting, and Claire's mother laughing at them, and the sounds of ordinary family happiness became unbearable and she rang off rather suddenly; and the silence and darkness came back again.

Nearly half-past six. Time to get dinner ready. She checked the fridge. Mrs Meggit had left cold meat and salad *again*.

She laid the table, banging down knives and forks as if she were thundering down brilliant forehands against Steffi. Through the open lounge door, as if from another planet, she heard the Wimbledon umpire's voice.

'Miss Graf wins six-love, six-love.'

And suddenly the smell from Mummy's room got too much for her. She crept upstairs to shut Mummy's door.

And had to look inside, like she always had to. Because if she didn't, she'd feel she was being rude to Mummy, not remembering her enough.

But it always looked the same. Mummy's bed made with great precision, as stiff and flat as a board. The array of bottles on the dressing-table, neat as the guards on parade. The huge mirrored wardrobe, still full of Mummy's elegant business gear.

She looked at herself, in Mummy's long mirror. At eighteen she was as tall as Mummy had been. Same slim build. But there the similarity ended. Mummy had had long silver-blonde hair, arranged six different ways a week. Lucy's hair was a dim mousy ghost of it, and always worn straight down her back, over a sloppy sweater. Mummy had been proud of her height, worn high heels to make herself look even taller; Lucy was ashamed of her height, and wore flatties to minimize it, and got told off for stooping. Lucy wore jeans all the time; nobody ever saw her legs, though in the privacy of undressing she sometimes thought her legs might one day become as good as Mummy's . . .

Mummy had been a magnificent butterfly; Lucy was a humble caterpillar who wanted to stay that way.

She turned from the mirror abruptly. To the wall where Mummy's favourite picture hung. The greatest antiques find their antique-hunting family had ever made. A tiny Rembrandt etching, bought with every penny that Mummy could borrow, when she was little more than a student. Mummy's first statement that she was going to be a glorious butterfly. Nobody had spotted it was a Rembrandt except Mummy. People, favoured people, were sometimes brought up here to see it . . .

Lucy's heart screwed up in agony.

Mummy's picture was gone. There was only the faintly darker patch on the wallpaper where it had been.

9

Lucy told herself to be sensible; maybe the picture had fallen off the wall, behind the bed.

But it wasn't there; it was gone, gone, gone.

Lucy felt like screaming her head off. Then she thought of ringing the police. Her hand was on the bedroom extension when something made her pause. It *couldn't* be a burglary, with the alarm still on and no sign of a break-in. It *must* be Daddy. Taking it to get it re-framed or something . . . but there was nothing wrong with the old frame. And why hadn't he *told* her? But even in her fluster, she felt uneasy about ringing the police, had a feeling that somehow Daddy wouldn't like that . . .

She would wait for him; he *couldn't* be much longer.

Drearily she wandered from room to room, making sure that all their other treasures were safe. Daddy's Ridgeway jugs, Mummy's precious Georgian tripod tables. The first antique Lucy had ever bought for herself, at the age of eleven: the spelter warrior they'd always called 'King Alfred the Great'. Mummy and Daddy had hovered protectively at a distance while little Lucy haggled with the dealer; had taken her to the post office in a strange holiday town, so she could draw out her money to pay for it.

Lucy fingered her own greatest-ever find, a pair of Regency rope-backs for eighty pounds, that even Mummy had envied. But that evening, nothing gave her pleasure or comfort. Everything felt far away from her. Like Daddy.

Finally she went and sat on the stairs, waiting for the sound of his step, of his key in the door. A thing she used to do years ago, when she was little and in trouble.

*

She was jolted out of a daze of misery by the sound of a key. The door opened, and for a dreadful moment she thought it was some stranger. Hunched . . . furtive. Then he turned his head to look back down the road, and she saw the light shine on his spectacles and the bald patch where his hair was thinning in front.

'Daddy!'

He gave a start and peered into the gloom of the hall.

'What's the matter, kitten? What you sitting there for?'

'The Rembrandt . . . it's gone!'

'Yes, I know,' he said gently. 'I sold it.'

'*Sold* it? But it was *Mummy's*!' Her voice rose to a screech at such a betrayal.

'Steady on, kitten. Let's go and sit down. Pour me my usual, and I'll put you in the picture.' His voice sounded utterly weary, and as if he was bracing himself for some long and difficult job. He went into the lounge, and slumped into the couch. Put down a briefcase beside him. Not his usual smart black one, but a much-scuffed stout leather one.

She poured him his usual, with hands that shook with rage. She banged it down on the occasional table beside him, so that it spilt a little.

'*Why* did you sell it? Are we hard up or something?' She had never been so angry with him. She sounded like Mummy at her worst.

He said, 'I want you to listen carefully,' and his tone took away all her rage and made her go weak at the knees, so that she dropped down on to the couch beside him. It was the same tone as he'd used to tell her Mummy was dead in a car-crash.

He took the briefcase on his knee and undid the three straps. Inside was more money than she'd ever seen. Bundles of tens and twenties and fifties, with elastic bands round them of different colours and thicknesses, yellow, blue, brown. The money was all dirty, and some notes were torn and mended with Sellotape. A slightly sour greasy smell of human hands came off them.

'This is the money from the Rembrandt,' he said. 'It's for you. It's your running-away money.'

'Running-away money?' She was totally baffled. 'Running-away money' was an old family joke. Mummy used to call her own bank account her 'running-away money'. Lucy when small had picked up the habit and called her post office savings the same. As if anyone would have dreamt of running away from someone as gentle as Daddy . . .

It had been a joke, but it was not a joke now. She looked at his grey face, at the little tic that made his left eyebrow flicker up and down so often these days . . . he was dead serious. She had a brief terror that he was going insane . . . but he was speaking quite clearly and logically, only a bit too fast in his anxiety.

'You must run away to somewhere where nobody can find you. You mustn't go to anybody you know. That's the first place they'll look. You mustn't even go to any place you've ever been on holiday. That's the second place they'd look. You mustn't even go to any place you'd like. You must go to some place you'll really hate – somewhere black and filthy and slummy would be best. Somewhere they'll *never* think of looking for you. And you must change your name, and your appearance if you can – your picture might be in the papers . . .'

It was all unbelievable. It wasn't happening. It *was* insane. And yet she half-believed it, because of the look on his face . . .

'Daddy,' she whispered through dry lips, grasping his hand. 'Daddy – *who* am I running away from?'

Chapter Three

He didn't answer for so long. She felt like grabbing him and shaking him. She felt like grabbing him and hugging him for comfort she was so scared.

But he had turned away, and was staring at the small marble bust of Queen Victoria on the mantelpiece at the far side of the room. Almost as if he was communing with the good old Queen. Then he finally said, 'I can't tell you any more. Or the police will be able to charge you with conspiracy . . .'

'*Police*?' If it had been unbearably bad before, it was unbearably worse now. 'Daddy, what have you *done*?' Her mind raced around wildly. Had he knocked down somebody with the car? Was he a hit-and-run? Had he stolen money? But what money was there to steal? Was it because he'd sold the Rembrandt? 'Daddy, you must *tell* me.'

'All I can tell you is that it's going to get pretty rough round here, and I want you out of it. Clear. Away. It won't just be the police. It'll be the media too. TV crews camped on our lawn. Paparazzi following you wherever you go. I've seen it. It gives people nervous breakdowns. I want you out, clear, away.'

'No,' she said. 'I'm not going. I'm staying with you, to look after you. I don't care about the paparazzi.' The last word felt strange on her tongue. She'd never said it before, just read it. 'I'm going to stay. We'll manage. We always do.'

13

As she said it, part of her mind, the cool detached part, said 'liar'. She wasn't really staying to look after him; she was clinging to him, more desperately than she ever had in her life . . .

As if he had sensed that last honest thought, he turned and looked at her. 'You must go. You can't help. You'd weaken me; I've got enough to worry about without worrying about you. If I know you're away and hidden and safe, that will help. That's the best thing you can do for me.'

She had to *know*, if she died for it. She had one desperate bargaining-counter, and she used it.

'I won't go; not unless you tell me what you've done!'

He looked at her sorrowfully. 'That's blackmail, kitten. You're blackmailing me.'

'I don't care. I *won't* go away, unless you tell me what you've done.' Terrible fear-phantoms crowded in on her. Had he killed somebody? Molested a child? All the unthinkable things.

Perhaps he sensed again what she was thinking. He put his face in his hands and said, 'Oh, God.' Which brought her again to the verge of panic.

Finally he said, in a low voice, 'It's not something I've done, kitten. It's something I'm *going* to do. It's nothing *nasty*. I'm not going to hurt anybody or kill anybody. Does that satisfy you?'

At first she felt a relief so enormous she could have wept. All the nightmare thoughts fled away. She felt almost normal, just terribly shaky.

But the trouble hadn't really gone away. It was still going to happen . . . 'the police' . . . 'nothing nasty' . . . And he worked nowhere near money . . . ?

Work. The Department. The things he would never talk about . . . Government secrets. New nightmares flew in on her . . .

14

'Daddy.' She gripped his hands again. 'It's not the Russians? It's not like . . . Kim Philby?'

He gave a strangled snort that might have been disgust or dreary strangled laughter. 'I'm not in the Foreign Office, kitten. Or the War House. Anyway, what are the Russkis now? No, nothing like Kim Philby. I'd make a lousy spy. I'm too scared.'

'Well . . . what? It is the Department, isn't it? You don't have to tell me. I *know*.' Then she added, with desperate cunning, 'Tell me it's not true then . . .'

His expression told her it was true. He rubbed his face with both hands, wearily. Then nodded, still looking at the good old Queen, and said at last, in a dreary drained voice, 'Our Lords and Masters in Whitehall have been very wicked, kitten. And I'm going to blow the whistle on them. The whole world will know. The whole world will hate us for it.'

'For *what*?' Oh, this was so like Daddy. Nothing criminal, nothing wicked, how could she ever have suspected that of Daddy, who wouldn't even get off a bus without paying his fare? But this, this was *so* typical. Always tell the truth, kitten! Tell the truth and shame the devil!

'Daddy, tell me what they've done!'

'No,' he said. And she knew she had come up against an iron gate, an unscalable cliff. 'No, if I told you, kitten, *you* would be a conspirator under the law, and you could go to prison too.'

'*Prison!*' How had she ever thought things were bad before?

'For years. When they catch me. *Now* do you see why you have to go away? The gutter press will want to eat the traitor's daughter alive. And if the police don't catch me in time, they'll come for you. You'll have MI5 interrogators at you for days on end – every detail of your life, and my life.

15

I know how foul they can be. I don't want them anywhere near you.'

'You don't *have* to do it.'

'Somebody has to.'

'Why does it have to be you?'

'Because I'm the only one who knows about it. I'm the only one that's spotted what they're up to. As far as I know. It's all hidden inside mounds and mounds of paper. Different departments inside the Department. Nobody sees the lot. A memo here, a report there. I've been searching for months . . . ever since Mummy died. It's the only thing that made it worthwhile going on . . .'

'There's ME! Aren't *I* worth going on for?'

He was silent after that. Hiding guilt inside silence. Desperately she used her little advantage.

'You don't *have* to do it. You could write to the papers, anonymously . . .'

'An anonymous letter is not proof. I'm still searching for the proof. And they can gag newspapers with the Official Secrets Act. As you very well know.'

'Daddy . . . ?'

He put his hand on her arm now. 'Lucy, look at me. Do you remember what I taught you, when you were little? The thing I told you was more important than anything else? The thing we've always said to each other?'

She knew the saying he meant. The Edmund Burke. She shook her head; she would not say it.

'Then I'll say it for you. "For evil to flourish, it is enough that good men do nothing."'

She shook her head mutely, eyes shut, tears pricking at her lids.

'Oh,' said her father, 'it's a grand saying to say, in easy times. It's a grand thing to put on classroom walls for children. It doesn't cost anything to do that. But the time is

16

now, Lucy. Like 1940 was the time for your grandfather. He did it, and didn't flinch. I'm going to do it. Are you with me, or against me, Lucy?'

She seemed to dwell a long time in some cold and lonely place, without air. But finally, almost against her will, she said, 'With you.'

'Bless you. I knew you wouldn't let me down.'

And with *that* saying, iron gates seemed to clang behind her back.

She said in a dreary voice, 'When do I have to go?' Desperately clutching for a day, two days . . .

'Tomorrow morning, kitten.'

'*Tomorrow?*' It was another knife driving into her heart.

'It's not safe to leave it later. At work . . . I'm drawing out more and more files that I never usually use. Files I have no real right to see. They watch out for that kind of thing in registry . . . the security people. They could be on to me already; just biding their time and watching, trying to find out who else is in it with me. I thought I was still in the clear, but I . . . fancied a car followed me home tonight. It turned off the main road half a mile away, but that doesn't mean anything, they pass you on from car to car . . . But I'm sure they won't be following you yet. Our Lords and Masters have a reluctance to pay police overtime.'

'How am I going to get *away*?'

'You can take Mummy's Volks. But dump it as soon as you can. Sooner or later the police will spot it's missing, and get its number off the Swansea computer. You must dump it at the far end of some big car park, a long way from where you're going to live . . . What were you going to do tomorrow morning?'

17

nnis with Claire.' But that had been another life, y as Ancient Rome . . .

....., carry on and do that. But after you've finished playing tennis, don't come back here. Pack your bags tonight and get them into the Volks. Then, after Claire, just take off into the blue. But keep an eye on your car mirror. Just make sure you aren't being followed . . .'

Followed? It was crazy. Like something out of a TV movie. Again she wondered if he was going mad, tipping over the edge. Losing Mummy, then all that work, work, work. Top civil servants in Whitehall did have nervous breakdowns, only they were hushed up. She looked at him warily. His face was very pale; he was sweating. That left eyebrow was never still. He had that stiffness round his mouth that made him work hard to speak clearly. But he didn't look *mad*. But then how could she tell what *was* mad . . . and there was no one to help, no one who would believe her. And defying him would just make him worse. She knew in her heart that, mad or sane, she would have to go. If he was just mad, then she could come back later and look after him again.

'I'll let you have more money, kitten, eventually. From the sale of this house, the antiques. I'll see you're all right . . .'

She wanted to shout, 'I don't want money. I want home, I want you!' But she just stared around at all the familiar things, that were her safe place, that she might never see again. They suddenly seemed as thin as cardboard, as thin as ghosts.

But already he was running on:

'There's thirty thousand in that briefcase. That should last you a bit. You can get well lost on thirty thousand . . .'

'*Thirty thousand*?' Under her dreary calm, panic began to

18

boil up again. How could she keep all that money safe? She eyed the briefcase in horror.

'Put it into building societies, kitten. Not more than two thousand at a time, or they'll notice. Start new accounts in your new name. In some town well away from where you're living. Look, I've written all the instructions down for you; about all the things you have to do; in case you forget something. I've had a lot of time to think this out; I don't think I've missed anything. But burn them as you finish with them . . .' He took a sheaf of notes out of the scuffed briefcase with a hand that trembled slightly. They were in his own spiky elegant handwriting, and on Whitehall memo-paper. Even in his treachery, he was the perfect civil servant, thought of everything . . .

She thought, you worked it all out. While we ate together, played tennis, bought antiques, were half-happy. And you never said a word to me. She had the bitter thought that he was betraying her, as well . . .

But he was Daddy. He was all she had. So she only said, 'When I get safe . . . how do I let you know?'

'It's in the notes – it's rather neat, that. We use the "In Memoriam" columns of the *Telegraph* – because we both dislike the *Telegraph* so much. Our code-word is "Nathaniel". You use it to send me the telephone number of where you're staying, and your false name. Suppose it's Sheffield 201157 . . . you put in the *Telegraph* something like, "In loving memory of Nathaniel Sheffield, died 20th November 1957, still missed by his grand-daughter Jane Bloggs." Got it?'

'But Daddy, that won't work for some numbers. Like "77" in the middle . . .'

'*Look!*' he said, and quite suddenly he was in a rage such as she'd never seen him in before. 'Look – *you* work something out. You're a bright girl – surely you can work the damn thing out for yourself? Do I have to *spoon-feed* you?'

She began to shake. 'Sorry! Sorry!'

But already his rage had passed, and he was his old gentle controlled self again.

'I'm sorry too, kitten. You've got enough to put up with, without me losing my rag. Sorry, kitten. Let's go and have some supper. It's gone eight. No point to plotting on an empty stomach, eh?'

Breathing unreal air through oddly tight lungs, she sat at the unreal dining-table and passed him the unreal salad, the very sight of which made her want to throw up.

Chapter Four

They spent one of the most dreadful evenings of their lives. Silences that seemed to drag on for ever, in which she listened to the sound of her father's breathing, then her own, every rustle as he moved in his chair or rattled the paper in a pretence of reading it. While the pressure inside her, to plead with him not to do it, mounted up and up till she could've screamed. And in between the silences there were bursts of frantic discussion, when they went over something again and again, until Daddy grew hoarse and impatient, and she, with her head in a whirl, was on the verge of tears. They even tried to get away from it by watching the news, but she couldn't remember a thing the newsreader said, and the rioting crowds and the rescued kidnap victim and the earthquake workers in Bolivia seemed empty pointless puppets.

Nothing worked. Nothing stopped her shaking, or her stomach rumbling. Every thing was worse than the last. Until, near midnight, he said, 'I think I'll turn in. I'll leave you to get your packing done. Don't sit up too late. You've got a big day tomorrow.'

He gave her a kiss; his lips were very dry and trembly. 'See you in the morning, before I go.' Close-to, she noticed that one of his eyes was bloodshot, and there was white dry stuff at the corners of his mouth.

In her heart of hearts, she was glad to see him go. She almost relaxed, as she listened to his weary footsteps dragging upstairs. She heard him go to the bathroom; heard the loo flush. Heard his bedroom door close, with a very final click. He would be taking his two, three, four sleeping pills, drugging himself out of this terrifying world until the morning, when he must face it again.

She must put no further burden on him. She was alone now. She sat and let the waves of her own terror break over her; noting with some surprise that one *could* break out in a cold sweat. Terror of leaving home; terror for Daddy; terror of that scuffed briefcase beside her. Above all, the terror of knowing she had no future, except what she made by her own wits, her own will-power.

She had no wits. She was clever at schoolwork. She could make people laugh, when she felt comfy and at home with them. But what good were schoolwork and jokes now?

And she had no will-power. She realized with a sickening thump that she had always done what other people wanted. Daddy, Mummy, teachers, friends. She was a doormat; and now a terrified doormat. And beyond Daddy loomed enormous things . . . She had always rather liked the Prime Minister, who looked kind and caring on the telly. She had had great faith in Parliament; had sympathized with the police who had a rotten job to do . . .

They were all the enemy now. And behind them, more scary because never seen, MI5.

She just sat and sat, and the thoughts chased each other through her mind, like hamsters on their wheel. Round and round and round. If only she could take sleeping pills like Daddy, and get away from them. But she mustn't sleep; she must *plan*.

Well, she could pack. At least she knew how to pack. She drearily went upstairs and got out her old suitcase and threw in pants and pyjamas and stuff. But when she came to other clothes, she despaired. All she had were washed-out jeans

22

and sloppy sweaters and anoraks. And that's what the police description would say . . . last seen wearing jeans and sloppy sweater and anorak. And it would say she always wore her hair straight down her back, and had blue eyes and was five feet ten. They might even show her photo on *Crimewatch*. Everybody watched *Crimewatch*. People got caught by the police within minutes of their photos appearing on the programme . . .

She had a sudden impulse to run round the house tearing up and burning every photograph of her that had ever been taken. But that was stupid. She'd had her photograph taken with the whole school, only two weeks ago. Claire had photographs of her, Aunt May and Aunt Grace had photographs of her . . .

She must change her whole appearance. But she stared at herself in her bedroom mirror, at her mousy hair, at her stomach sticking out despairingly, at her eyes, over-wide tonight with shadows under them. Hopeless weak doormat face . . .

But looking in the mirror reminded her . . . She had looked in a mirror earlier today; a longer mirror.

Mummy's mirror. Then it hit her like a clap of thunder.

Mummy's wardrobe.

Mummy's clothes, shoes, underwear, snazzy coloured tights. Elegant worldly witty snooty Mummy, with her hair up in a chignon on top of her head, and her long white neck.

She had watched Mummy so often, putting up her chignon; helped her. Once Mummy had even shown her how to do it.

Could she still manage it?

Wild with some sudden delirious crazy hope, she tiptoed to Mummy's room. After what seemed hours of desperate fiddling with hairpins, she had it. A little ragged and lopsided, but it would do. She had the trick of it; practice would make perfect. She snatched one of Mummy's last suits from the wardrobe and tried it on. It was just a little loose. Mummy, in spite of rigid dieting, had never quite managed the teenage figure she'd wanted. But again, the suit would do.

Mummy's set of matched designer luggage. The weltering luxury of Mummy's silk blouses and underwear. Everything. It was like breaking into a holy temple, a queen's cold tomb. But Mummy wouldn't have minded. She'd have laughed, in her cynical way . . .

Finally she chose her outfit for tomorrow and put it on. Her image stared back at her out of the mirror. A power-dressed young woman in her early twenties; a younger version of Mummy. Who would speak in Mummy's imperious way, have Mummy's elegant gestures.

A final thought struck her. Mummy's reading spectacles. Not that Mummy ever let anybody see her wearing reading spectacles; but being Mummy's they were in the very latest style. And their lenses were so weak that Lucy, putting them on one evening for a joke, had found she could actually see pretty well through them; even if they blurred things ever so slightly.

The image stared back; now even a little intimidating. It would do; she could face the world as *that*.

She carried the suitcases out to the car, without putting on the lights again downstairs. Thank God the garage was linked to the kitchen by an internal door.

When she had loaded the Volks, she peeped out through the little broken pane in the garage door. The road was empty of people under its street-lights, but there were dark cars parked and she couldn't see inside them. *Were* they watching?

She shuddered and went to bed.

She finally slept, towards dawn. Still dozing, not wanting

to move, not wanting to leave her last warm safe place, she heard Daddy get up, shower. Finally, her bedroom door opened, and he peeped in on her. In the dim, curtained light, he looked *so* tired.

She reached an arm out of bed, and they touched fingers.

'Best of luck, kitten!'

'Best of luck, Daddy.'

They were fellow-conspirators now.

He gave her a kiss; he smelt of the usual aftershave. But he had cut himself shaving; there was a dry fleck of dark blood, with a tiny tuft of white sticking to it.

She listened to his car going down the road, till it was lost in the distant roar of the morning traffic.

'Well, what got into *you*?' asked Claire, as she flopped down on the bench of the tennis court, red and sweating, and shoved her racket back in her Adidas bag. 'Going in for Wimbledon next year or something?'

'Don't know,' said Lucy shortly. The brilliant way she had played didn't make sense to her, either. After three hours sleep and all that frenzied panic, she ought to have played like a wet lettuce. But it had been good to hit, hit, hit. Like she was hitting an enemy. She felt a little light-headed, terribly alive and as high as a kite. She only hoped it wouldn't wear off, with everything she had to do.

She drove Claire home, resisting the urge to chatter like a magpie, and watching in the driving-mirror all the way for cars which might be following her. So that she once nearly rammed the car in front at some traffic-lights. That brought out one of her cold sweats – that was the worst thing that could happen; a damaged car; having to talk to policemen.

But she didn't quite hit the car in front; a matter of inches. And nothing *seemed* to be following her. But that didn't mean much. She'd watched too many episodes of *The Bill*. She knew they could follow from in front; talk to each other over their radios.

But there didn't seem to be any cars driving in front of them either. And Claire's shadowed leafy road didn't have a car in sight, apart from housewifely Fiat Pandas and Renault Fives parked in driveways.

'Coming in for something long and cool?' asked Claire.

Lucy considered. Sometimes when she played Claire she did go in for a drink; sometimes she didn't. Above all, she wanted to act *normal*. Though Claire didn't know it yet, she was going to be the last person to see the old Lucy alive. Claire would have to answer the policeman's questions. But she would like that; she liked a bit of drama; maybe she would have *her* picture in the papers, or get on telly. Goodoh for Claire.

But meanwhile, if she had to sit acting normal in Claire's house for another hour, she'd go bananas . . .

'Don't think I will,' she said carefully. 'I'm all sweaty. I need a shower. I'll get along home.'

She wished next second she hadn't said that. Because she wasn't going home; wasn't going to get a shower. And she needed a shower more than anything. The need for a shower, the need for home came down on her mind like the sudden dark of a thunder-cloud.

Claire got out, fussing with her sweat-dark hair.

'Shower – bliss! Goodbye, tiger. Same time tomorrow?'

'Same time tomorrow,' said Lucy, and drove off feeling like Judas.

She drove north out of London up the M1, feeling as exposed as a fly on a white table-cloth, glowering at the police traffic cars that hung overhead on flyovers and slip-roads. None seemed to pay the slightest attention to her. As far as she could see.

Fifty miles on, she turned off and went to the old picnic-place, a little stretch of country that Mummy and Daddy had loved for picnics more than any other. But that wasn't why she had chosen it. She'd chosen it because it was an interlacing network of tiny roads, meeting at all angles and with very few signposts so that even Mummy and Daddy sometimes got lost. Mummy had always called it the Bermuda Triangle . . .

She drove backwards and forwards across it, for nearly half an hour, till she was thoroughly lost herself. The tiny cottages, and green patches under the shade of trees, whizzed past her time and again; she felt as if she was somehow abusing them, beating them to death, ruining the old happy memories of them.

She saw few cars, and they were mud-spattered and farmerish. The rest was Land-rovers and tractors, a bus full of grannies and two delivery vans.

Finally convinced she wasn't being followed, she pulled off up a little green lane, and waited, with the doors open, to cool down. It was shady and peaceful under the trees. She felt safe, like a child rocked in a green shady rustling cradle.

She must have fallen asleep. For suddenly a voice was asking, demanding, 'Are you all right?'

She opened her eyes in terror. It was a man with a balding, sweating head, and a small paunch bulging out his red-and-white striped shirt with its white collar.

'Are you all right?' he said again.

'Yes – I was just tired, so I must have fallen asleep.'

'Not a good idea, with your doors wide open like that,' said the man. 'You don't know who might have come along. There's some funny people about these days.'

His eyes swivelled away from her, to stare at the bonnet of the Volkswagen.

Funny people? He meant rapists. She looked at herself, at her long bare legs sprawled any old how, at the buttons of her tennis shirt, with one too many undone.

'Sorry,' she said, gathering herself together.

'You're lucky I'm an old married man,' he said, bitterly. 'With three kids and a mortgage.' There was anger in his voice. He had looked at her, while she was sprawled asleep. He had been tempted . . .

'Thanks a lot,' she said.

'I should think on, in future, if I were you.' He stalked back to his car, a Ford Sierra, with his coat hung on a hanger over the back seat, and brown boxes on the back shelf. A commercial traveller . . . or a policeman disguised as a commercial traveller? No, he was too little for a policeman. He was only about five feet six. Policemen had to be five feet ten; the careers teacher had said so. Five feet ten for men, and five feet five for women.

But perhaps that didn't apply to MI5.

She sat on another hour, as the day cooled. Then she went and found a little tinkling stream, and washed herself. Then changed into Mummy's gear within the green shade of a tree whose branches came right down to the ground. By the time she was changed, she was sweating again, and she snagged her tights slightly on a broken branch. She sat in the car, using the wide rear-mirror to put up her chignon. When she had finished, she thought she looked *nothing* like elegant Mummy. But with the spectacles on, she didn't look like herself either. Something in between . . .

Tonight, she must sign in at an hotel. By tonight, she must have a new name. Something as near the truth as possible, Daddy had said; the best lies were always those closest to the truth.

28

She took out her driving licence and looked at it. Another danger-point.

LUCY RACHEL KING SMITH, it said. Funny, she was Rachel as well as Lucy. But she'd never felt like a Rachel. Nobody had ever called her Rachel since the day she was born. She kept forgetting about Rachel altogether, except when she had to fill in forms. So Rachel it would be. That was easy; she was stealing nothing. She *was* a Rachel really.

But the surname was the important part. It was the surname that would get her into trouble; that would be on all the computers the police would look at. She *must* be the same, but she *must* be different . . .

Then suddenly she gave a wild giggle. She reached into the glove-compartment and got out a black Biro, and carefully, with a shaking hand, drew a small bar between 'King' and 'Smith'.

Lucy Smith had become Rachel King-Smith. And in time, the way she said it to people, Rachel Kingsmith. It was smart; it went with her new image. 'King' would mean nothing to the police: it was her granny's maiden name. Nobody else in the family had ever used it.

Much heartened, the new Rachel Kingsmith drove off. Keeping off the motorways, with their police traffic cars. Along tiny winding roads that led on and on and on. North.

North. Smoke. Shabbiness. Unemployment. She hated them all. And the smokiest, shabbiest, biggest place she could think of.

Manchester.

It seemed utter luxury, simply to know again who she was, and where she was going.

She wanted to stay somewhere small, obscure, down-at-heel, where no one would notice her.

But that was Lucy Smith, typical Lucy Smith. Therefore she must do the opposite. Somewhere big, somewhere lush, somewhere grand, in the city centre.

She found it.

The reception-clerk summed her up as she came in. Money, in the clothes, in the Gucci handbag. A business-woman, from the well-used briefcase. Young and pretty sexy, but tired to death. These Yuppies certainly made their loot young; but they paid the price. Still, it was his job to keep them happy. Yes, madam, dinner can be served in your room. Yes, madam, I'll get someone to park your car in the underground car park. Room forty-four, madam. I'll have your luggage sent up.

Up in forty-four, she kicked off her shoes, which were just a little too tight, and collapsed on the bed.

She was asleep when the dinner came; but she managed to give the right sort of tip, when she found her handbag.

Chapter Five

She came awake with a rush in the strange room; her heart pounded; she was sweating; she felt sick. She sat up too quickly, and her head went swimmy for a moment. Then she just sat there, trying to feel better, and rubbing her legs and shoulders to ease aches and pains that seemed to have invaded every part of her.

She sat in the middle of her own clutter. Half-closed suitcases, with things hanging out of them; her clothes a draggled heap on the chair. But beyond the personal draggle, the room offered her nothing. An impersonal box with boring wallpaper and the usual boring furniture, and a mass-produced print by David Shepherd, of elephants walking in a glade with shafts of sunlight. Through a half-open door was the other impersonal box of the bathroom.

Then she saw the telly, its gray glaucous dead eye staring at her. It was nearly time for a news. There might be something about Daddy. She staggered across and fumbled desperately with the unfamiliar buttons on the control box. The newsreader swam up; the news had started, but only the headlines.

There was nothing about Daddy; but then there wouldn't be, would there? MI5 would keep very quiet if they arrested Daddy.

But switching on the telly had got her moving. She made herself a cup of tea, washed, cleaned her teeth. Each action seemed to be like putting on a tiny piece of armour, made life a little more bearable. By the time her chignon was up (and rather better, this time) she was in the full set of armour that was Rachel Kingsmith.

She must face breakfast. She must eat whenever she could. Plenty. As a discipline, like she must now go to the loo whenever a chance came. But as she reached for the door-handle, the briefcase with the money glowered at her. She daren't leave it here. She didn't know when the cleaning woman would come to do her room. They might come during breakfast. And cleaning women were always nosy . . .

She'd take it down to breakfast. Why shouldn't she? What did it matter what the waitress thought? She was being paid, wasn't she? To hell with her . . .

The waitress stared at the briefcase, but only with respect. Suddenly triumphant, Lucy ordered a huge breakfast, the whole works. Then found she didn't know what to do with her eyes and her hands. Glancing round surreptitiously, she saw other people, eating on their own, were reading newspapers. How stupid of her; she'd seen spare newspapers on the registration desk in the hall. She must nip back for one. Leaving the briefcase?

She made a quick dash.

'A paper, madam?'

She almost said *The Times* from habit. But Daddy got *The Times* . . . She settled for *The Independent* instead. She must learn to be independent now, she thought wildly.

She came back to find the waitress staring at her empty table and abandoned briefcase, in bafflement. Then the woman saw her paper and smiled. 'Nice to have something to read when you're on your own, miss!' She had a friendly voice.

It was as she finished her bacon and eggs that Rachel felt somebody else staring at her, from three tables away. Surreptitiously, she examined him over the rim of her paper.

32

A tall young man, long legs stuck out in immaculate grey suiting, gelled fair hair, snub nose. Then the young man looked across again and smiled at her, a very friendly I-know-you sort of smile. She gave him what might have passed for a vacant grin back. She didn't know him from Adam. Then she fled back to her paper.

But every time she looked towards him, he grinned the same confident grin again. Who on earth *was* he? Some young colleague of Daddy's, brought home to dinner years ago? Some old boy from school? Was her disguise *that* bad? Surely this wasn't the way MI5 went on? Besides, his suit was far too good for him to be a policeman . . .

God, he was coming over . . . She made herself survey him with eyes levelled like a sword. He had a few freckles across his nose. It was a pity that her spectacles had slid down her own suddenly sweaty nose, leaving her eyes naked.

'Nick Smart,' he said, holding out a large paw. 'ICI Pharmaceuticals.'

She took the hand because she didn't know what else to do. And said, 'Rachel Kingsmith' for the very first time, apart from signing her name in the hotel register.

'Dump, isn't it?' he said cheerfully, looking round the dining-room. 'I don't intend to ruin my digestion by dining here tonight. I don't suppose you'd care to eat out with me; take mercy on a benighted stranger . . .'

God, he was trying to pick her up! His impish glance was not on the briefcase, but on her Gucci handbag, her legs looking elegant in Mummy's tights. She was so relieved she almost gave in to him. Just in time she said, 'I'm leaving today. I've got to be in . . . Milan . . . first thing tomorrow morning.'

Too late she realized she was impersonating that woman on the coffee ad.

But he just shrugged his shoulders, with impish regret, and said, 'I'm going to Glasgow. Too bad about tonight. I know some good restaurants in this old town. Some other time, then. Have a good day.' And then he was striding away, as bouncy as ever.

But somehow it cheered her. He hadn't taken her for a droopy eighteen-year-old. He didn't look the kind of man who needed to pick up droopy eighteen-year-olds. He'd treated her as a woman of the world.

It gave her courage for the next step: the building societies. She counted the money into piles on the bed, ear constantly cocked for the cleaning-women coming. Then she riffled the stationery stock on her writing-desk for envelopes, and marked the envelopes '£1000' or '£1500' or '£2000'. Put the money in and tucked down the flaps. She had to do the last few in a rush, as she heard the cleaning-women's clanking approach. Five envelopes into her handbag, the rest into her briefcase, a quick false smile and 'good morning' to the women, and away off to the lift.

The first building society was totally empty. Every idle counter-clerk watched her all the way in from the door. For a horrible moment, she couldn't decide which of them to choose; then hurled herself towards the smallest and meekest-looking girl. She offered the first envelope. The girl shook her head in a baffling terrifying way. Waved her hand negligently to refuse the envelope. Lucy's world began to rock around her. Then the girl glanced sideways and downwards. There was a little block of polished wood on the counter, saying quite clearly 'Position Closed'. The girl was otherwise occupied, tapping the keys of her computer.

Along the counter, somebody sniggered. Blindly Lucy scurried to the next position. A young man.

34

'Had a rough night last night, eh?' said the young man.

Lucy gaped at him in horror; how could he know? This was a nightmare. The world was no longer sane.

'I mean . . . a bit too much to drink,' said the young man. 'At a party or something . . . I mean you . . .' As Lucy went on gaping at him in paralysed horror, he became embarrassed; then actually blushed himself. It took all the will Lucy had left to jab the envelope at him. They were all still staring at her, wondering.

The young man fell to counting the notes. Lucy just stood watching him, the blood pounding through her head.

'There's twenty pounds too much here,' said the young man, looking up at last. 'The envelope's marked "£1000" and there's £1020. Do you want the twenty back or shall I put it in with the rest?'

She couldn't decide; she couldn't make her mouth work.

Then she heard the girl she had just left say to the girl next to her, 'Wasn't much of a do last night, was it? I thought the food was awful. That prawn cocktail . . .'

'I didn't have it,' said the other girl. 'I didn't like the look of it. I had melon instead. But that's the last leaving-do we have *there*.'

They weren't taking a blind bit of notice of Lucy; their minds had turned elsewhere. And the girl beyond them was busy examining her nail-varnish . . .

'Put it in with the rest,' said Lucy, as hope returned and she took a deep deep breath. 'And I'm opening a new account. My name is Rachel King-Smith.' Then gave the street number of her hotel as her address. Nobody ever thought of grand hotels as having street numbers; but they were always there somewhere in the entrance lobby. She'd noticed as she left the hotel that morning.

Five minutes later, she was outside with her brand-new pass-book in her hands, in the name of Rachel King-Smith.

She fled to the nearest ladies, locked herself in a cubicle, and counted out the contents of all her envelopes all over again, with sweaty fingers, dreading she might hear a loud knocking on the cubicle door, an imperious female voice demanding to know what she was doing in there and why she was being so long . . .

But female footsteps just came and went, and female voices only talked about aching feet and delinquent husbands and how full the shops were, with the summer sales. Blessed, blessed boring voices . . .

And after that, it got easier. Yes, the counter-clerks sometimes stared at her; but the women's eyes were only on her clothes and bag, and the men's gaze always started with her legs . . . The building societies seemed to come in clusters of five or six, for some reason. She had the nasty thought that all the building society workers might have lunch together, and would perhaps discuss over their meal the weird girl who had put thousands of pounds into each of them, one after another, that morning. Till she heard a gassy fat female customer drawing out three thousand to pay for her family holiday in Thailand, and telling all the world her business. Then she knew that she, Lucy, was very small beer indeed, and in some danger of getting paranoid.

By lunchtime, with nineteen pass-books in her briefcase, and only four thousand pounds left in her bag, she suddenly realized she was footsore, and very hungry indeed. She went into a pizzeria and ordered her favourite pizza, medium size.

But no sooner had one burden departed than another reared its ugly head.

The car. Still in the hotel's underground car park. How soon would the police spot it was missing from the double-garage at home? Once they got its number from the Swansea computer, every policeman in the country would be watching out for it . . .

She had the car brought up from the garage, and cruised the inner-city car-sales lots. Daddy had told her what to look for. A place that sold second-hand cars already RAC-tested. Eventually she found one, boasting its RAC tests with big flaring banners. She drove on a hundred yards and parked, and walked back shaking only slightly. This was the big test. Car-salesmen were sharp-eyed sharks; not unsuspecting sheep like building society girls.

She tried to wander through the ranked cars nonchalantly. Looking for something ordinary, middle-aged, with a long road fund and long MOT, just as Daddy had said.

The salesman was on to her in a flash.

'Can I help you, madam?' Eyeing her legs; again. Did men think of nothing but women's legs? Yes, their Gucci handbags. The man's eyes glinted speculatively. Money, money, money.

'I don't want to be pestered while I'm looking,' she said. 'I'll call you when I need you.' And her spurt of anger made it come out snooty . . .

'Suit yourself,' said the salesman. And went on watching her through the big plate-glass window of the garage, chain-smoking.

She settled on an E-reg Metro in the end, a dull grey car that looked as if nobody had ever loved it. Priced at £2800. A real droopy-Lucy car. But she could hardly afford a car that went with the Rachel image. Rachel would have had a purple Lamborghini or something. She went back and, still playing it at her most snooty, demanded sight of the RAC test-report; and read it right to the end with great thoroughness.

'Everything been put right?'

'Yeah. Want a run in her?' He looked too eager; the

hand-on-the-knee-in-mistake-for-the-gear-lever   type.   He
was little and fat, his coat-button done up and bulging. His
hair was greasy, he had BO and he must be pushing fifty.
But he still thought he was God's gift.

She had to go through with it. She kept him at bay by
driving so viciously at the start of the Manchester rush-hour
that it was him who broke out in a cold sweat, and began
moaning about his ulcer.

'Christ,' he said, when they got back. 'You female Nigel
Mansells . . .'

Now came the moment. The moment she had to offer
cash because she daren't sign a cheque. And there was only
one reason for cash he'd understand.

'Twenty-eight hundred,' she said briskly. 'By cheque?'

'Yeah.'

'How much discount for cash? Notes in your hand?'

He gulped. And took the bait. Cash meant he could hide
the sale from the Income Tax people. And the VAT . . .

'I can let you have a hundred off,' he said, his eyes turning
suddenly greedy.

'No way,' she said. 'If you can't do better than that, I'll
go elsewhere . . .' She got out of the car, and picked up her
handbag from the back seat, and began to walk away.

'Twenty-six hundred,' he shouted after her. She kept on
walking, but not very fast.

'Twenty-five,' he shouted despairingly.

She hesitated dramatically for a moment, as if consider-
ing, then turned back.

'Twenty-four fifty,' she said. 'And I want it fully serviced
and a full tank of petrol. *And* I want it washed and polished.
By tomorrow morning at eleven.'

That was how Daddy used to talk to them. Mummy had
no need to; they were all over her, waiting to fulfil her
slightest whim.

'Bloody hell,' he said despondently. 'Women are worse than bloody men these days. They won't let you *live*.'

She left five hundred deposit. And again gave her address as the number of the hotel.

'You live posh. That's near the Grand, isn't it?'

'Next door but one,' she said coolly. 'New flats.'

'It's OK for some,' he said bitterly.

'Eleven tomorrow, or the deal's off.'

She heard him mutter 'Stuck-up cow' as she walked away.

The sweetest praise couldn't have pleased her more. Mummy would have been proud of her.

Once back in the Volks, she allowed herself the luxury of collapsing over the steering wheel for five whole minutes.

After three, a homely little woman was tapping on her windscreen asking anxiously if she was all right.

She lay awake and fretted where to dump the Volks. Not on some posh suburban street, for the Home Watch warden would report it, and then the police would know. Not in some inner-city suburb, for there it would be vandalized and the police would know. Not in a pub car park, or the landlord would report it. Not by a supermarket or the manager would report it. The big main car parks were out, and the cinema car parks. She was in terror of joyriders, for Mummy's poor little Volks. There seemed no place in the world where she could park a car . . .

At two a.m., the city grew as quiet as it would ever get. The shouting drunks lessened, and the screeching tyres, the sirens that might be police or fire or ambulance. Only the central heating hummed and waterpipes gurgled where some other poor soul, denied sleep, found other occupation . . .

And above it all, the sound of one big jet air-liner, as its engines screamed to gain height. And blissfully, the solution came to her. Ringway Airport. Long-stay car park. It would cost the earth. But it was worth it. And a handy taxi back to the city. She rolled over, and slept like a lamb.

Chapter Six

A week later, she reached the end of her tether. She parked the Metro high up a little valley that led on to the open moor; on a small rubbly car park that had fine open views, and a concrete litter-bin that strewed tourist crisp bags in all directions. She carefully crossed a sagging rusty wire fence, and sat on the banks of a little stream. Even here the litter had reached. Bovril flavour . . . Ready Salted . . .

She was hoping the sound of the little stream would soothe her; in the old days it always had. A mere week ago, she'd have dangled her bare feet in it, enjoying the feel of the water running between her toes. But Rachel Kingsmith couldn't afford to do that kind of thing; Rachel Kingsmith was even sitting on her headscarf to avoid getting green stains on her suit. Rachel Kingsmith the elegant clotheshorse was a bore.

And a total flop. She hadn't found a place to live. She'd driven as far north as the Lake District and as far east as the Vale of York. So many lovely houses; all with their front doors firmly shut. It wasn't just a matter of having money, even if you only wanted to rent. People didn't trust the young with property. House agents wanted references. Respectable married house agents probed pruriently about live-in lovers and all-night parties and even made absurd cutting jokes about acid-house romps. One man had offered her a dingy flat in Skipton, but stood too close to her when they went to inspect it.

And as for staying in hotels . . . you just had to gobble your meals and stay in your room watching telly, with the phone tempting you, tempting you from the corner; to phone Daddy at home which you must never do. Till you could bear the weight of that phone no more, and flung yourself out on late-night walks or drives, which drew suspicious nosy looks from the staff on the desk. Or went to bed and cried yourself to sleep; silently, for fear the person in the next room would hear and come and do a good Samaritan act. For people in hotels had too much time on their hands, were so nosy. At least the men were only flirty-nosy (you weren't even safe with the ones with bald heads). But the women . . .

'What's a pretty young thing like you doing on your own, my dear?' And it was no good just saying you were on holiday, because they asked what you did when you weren't on holiday. If you said college, they asked *which* college. And if you named a college, they always knew somebody, the friend of a daughter, or the daughter of a friend, who was at that college or had just left it. She had had several narrow escapes . . .

And if you said you were in business, it was what *kind* of business? And if you said antique-dealing (which was the only business you knew anything about) they said, 'You're very *young* to be an antique-dealer.'

To the last woman she had snapped, 'Sorry – I'll just nip off and dye my hair grey,' and swept out of the lounge. That would get her talked about. They *were* starting to talk at her present hotel; she was getting noticed. She would have to move on yet again. She could've wept.

Also, she was getting into the habit of coming up this particular valley too much. And sitting trying to soothe herself at the end of yet another pointless day. It was a mucky, spoilt little valley. The stone walls between the fields

42

were black, and the sheep were nearly as sooty. Too close to the smoke of Manchester, Leeds and Huddersfield. The fields were green enough (though God alone knew how much soot the sheep swallowed with their grass). But there had been a coal mine here once, and quarries, and the scars were left, precariously sealed off behind rusting barbed wire. And the village below her was beginning to die, with a few houses boarded up, and slates starting to strip from the roofs. Not a place for holiday cottages and second homes. Soot, and a network of power cables crossing the fields like iron spiderwebs were a good cure for holiday cottages . . .

Of course she knew why she came here too often. Down in the village, there was an antique-shop. The sort she and Daddy loved. No fitted carpets or tricksy spot-lighting. Just a dark cavern full of a tangle of interesting shapes, with a few battered chairs and old hall-stands on the pavement outside. The kind of place you could find bargains, if you kept your eyes open. It drew her, like a freshly baked pie draws a starving dog.

But she must *never* go there. If the police began enquiring among her teachers and friends, the first thing they'd tell them was that she was mad on antiques. It would be a very bad mistake indeed to go down there . . .

The sun went in. She felt a few spots of rain on the back of her hand. As she ran for the safety of the car, a fresh wave of despair hit her. Nothing to look forward to but another night being tormented by the silent waiting phone, another day of hopeless searching and insults.

She drove back slowly through the village, her windscreen wipers massacring the big spots of rain on the glass.

There were lights on in the antique-shop. Only bare bulbs, and yet they made the place look . . . homely, cosy even.

What the hell, she thought. What does it matter? I'm

43

going to fail anyway. I'm entitled to a bit of fun. She slammed the brakes on.

As she walked back, she realized that what she had thought of as being one long antique-shop was actually two. But the nearest one was dead, dark, empty, with only one old chair and a few crumpled sheets of newspaper in the window.

She walked into the living shop; an old-fashioned buzzer sounded above her head, and would not stop sounding, even when she pressed the door tight shut. It sounded like a giant iron bumblebee; it sounded like the end of the world. Desperately she tried opening the door, and banging it shut again.

'Drat the thing,' said a female voice. She spun round, and a face of unearthly beauty swam out of the darkness at the back of the shop. Tragic beauty really, for though the eyes were huge, dark and lovely, and the bone structure exquisite, there were lines on the face; lines of despair, almost hunger-lines, like a refugee-photograph.

'Here,' said the voice again. 'You see that mallet on that little table? Give it a bang wi' that.'

Lucy picked up the mallet; she thought it was an old croquet-mallet, the sole survivor of a once-elegant set. She tapped the dome of the buzzer sharply. It had no effect.

'No,' advised the voice behind her. 'Hit it a right whack. Like it was yer husband coming home drunk.'

Heart in her mouth, Lucy hit it a right whack.

It shut up at once.

'It needs seein' to,' said the voice. 'Like everything else round here.'

The beautiful tragic face emerged from the gloom. The body below was clad in a black sweater and washed-out blue jeans. It was painfully thin, and bent double under the

44

enormous load of a pine kitchen cupboard; like an ant in a nature film, carrying ten times its own weight.

'Here, let me help,' said Lucy, rushing forward.

'S'alright. Don't get yer suit dirty, love. It's all a matter of getting the point o' balance. There's a trick to it. I've carried things twice the weight of this.'

And, amazingly, the cupboard slid safely to the floor. The woman straightened, put her hands to her slender back and gave a two-handed squeeze. Then she pulled out a half-smoked cigarette and lit it, coughed once, and said, 'It's only the fear of lung cancer that keeps me goin'.'

Then she added, 'Have a look round, if you can get. Only mind that nice suit of yours – I'm not insured.'

Lucy, suddenly embarrassed, looked round wildly, and latched on to a china figure of Little Red Riding Hood, sitting on some impossibly bright green grass and cuddling a wolf so small he might have been a lap-dog. She'd seen the type before, but this was the biggest and best-modelled she'd ever seen. She felt a terrible urge to buy it; Daddy had been looking for a good one for years. But in her mind, she heard Daddy's cautioning voice: 'Check for cracks, darling, count the fingers. It's too late, once you've bought it.'

She took it to the window, to get the best light possible. Checked the hands, the wolf's nose, the sprigged grass, the places damage always occurred. She turned it upside down and saw that the price ticket, very grubby and half falling off, said twenty pounds. It was already a bargain, if there was no damage. Over and over she turned it, feeling for roughnesses and sharpnesses, with the soft sensitive tips of her fingers. But there was no damage, and the crackle of the glaze was dirty, as it should be. And the face was well painted with deft lively brushstrokes, as Staffordshire should be. Ten minutes elapsed, and still she looked for snags.

'You're in the trade, are you?' said the woman. There was a new respect in her voice, and the start of something that might have been friendliness.

'What's the best price you can do me?' said Lucy, without looking up. That was the phrase the dealers used. Only the ignorant asked for a discount, or something off.

'Seventeen's the best I can do,' said the woman. 'I paid fourteen for it.'

'I'm paying in notes,' said Lucy.

'Sixteen, then,' said the woman. Lucy nearly giggled, wondering how the Income Tax and VAT people ever got any money at all.

'I'll take it,' she said, putting it on the woman's shabby desk. 'But I'll go on looking round.'

'Mind that lovely suit,' said the woman again.

Lucy was lost in a maze of wonder. All the stuff was dirty, cobwebbed, rusty. But there was no rubbish, no modern repros like you got down south. It looked like it had all come out of local cottages. Kitchen scales, billhooks honed-down to sickle-moon thinness, three-legged stools with the dried cowmuck of the byres still sticking to the legs. A lovely wooden rocker, with the patina of a hundred years of greasy backsides. Lucy really wanted that. This was ridiculous. She had hardly enough room in the Metro for her own luggage, and . . .

'I can do you the chair for sixty,' said the woman. 'I can tell you fancy it.'

'But they're three times that price down south . . .'

'Aye well,' said the woman. 'The south's the south. They've got no sense down there, all them Yuppies. Ship the stuff down there, you'd make a fortune.'

'That's what I'm thinking,' said Lucy. A crazy idea was

46

growing in her mind. She asked, very casually, 'What happened to the shop next door?'

'Liz's? She packed up six months ago, when the new by-pass was opened. Killed her trade dead. She was all passing-trade you see. The Sunday-afternoon lot, from Leeds and Huddersfield off to the Lakes. Little rosy jugs, and all that sort of stuff. I'm hanging on, 'cos I mainly sell to other dealers, an' they know where to find me. Not that I shall be hanging on much longer, the state trade's in . . .'

'But you've got some lovely stuff . . .'

The woman's face lit up for a moment, and looked utterly beautiful. Then she said, 'S'all the bloody men. The Oldham and Rochdale lot. They keep on and on at you, till they just wear you down, and you give in at their price just to get rid of them.'

'Who owns the shop next door?'

'Old Bartlett.' The woman frowned. 'You thinkin' of takin' it? But you wouldn't do no trade, a lady like you. Stuff all polished and that, like Liz had. Them fellers used to have her in *tears*.'

'I wouldn't try to sell to them,' said Lucy stoutly. 'I'd move it down south, when I had enough . . .'

'Oh, well, if you've got a shop down there . . .' The woman sounded both deeply respectful and touchingly hopeful. 'I could do with some company. I've been bored out of me mind, since Liz went. You know what it's like, on yer own. I'll have a word wi' old Bartlett, if you like. He'll be glad of the money, poor old sod. He's long past it.'

'I'll take the rocker,' said Lucy, trying to stem her mad euphoria. 'And this hall-stand . . . ?'

'Thirty to you,' said the woman, brightening again. 'If you go on like this, us'll have bacon for tea tonight, any road.'

*

47

'Old Bartlett wants fifty pounds a week, rates included,' said the woman, when Lucy went back to the shop the following morning. 'I've got the keys. D'you want to have a look at it?'

They went in, lowering their voices like conspirators.

'One thing,' said the woman, 'the roof doesn't leak. But there's definitely mice and mebbe rats. You could do wi' a cat – a good ratter. Our Jim's goin' to drown our Tibbie, but he's not done it yet.'

'Why's he going to drown her?' asked Lucy, horrified.

'She's had kittens again. That's what they do round here. Keep the best she-kitten, and drown the rest and drown the mother. And she's a reet good ratter is Tibbie . . .' The woman seemed beyond sadness, beyond outrage. 'I sometimes wonder if one day our Jim won't drown me, if the shop goes bust. I'm good for nowt else – I had my hysterectomy two years ago.'

'But how old are you?' asked Lucy, and then stopped aghast at her rudeness. Though the woman didn't seem to mind in the least.

'Thirty-eight next birthday, and don't tell me; I look fifty.'

'I don't think you look fifty,' gasped Lucy. 'I think – you've got a marvellous face . . . like a ballerina or something.'

'Thanks a lot,' said the woman. 'But try telling my lot that. They'd laugh all the way to the pub.' She pushed on through the shop. 'There's a kitchen in the back. You could make yourself a cup of tea, if you get the electric put back on. An' there's an outside toilet in working order, if the local lads haven't been at it for the lead piping. One thing, Liz had a good strong back door fitted, an' bars over the back windows. You shouldn't have much trouble wi' burglars.'

'Have *you* had burglars?'

48

'They don't bother me, love. I take me petty cash home every night. They'd need a removal van to make a profit out of my stuff.'

'You don't live over the shop, then?'

'Love yer, no. Wouldn't live in this dump. We gotta house up Barnston. But there's three rooms up here that's handy for storage.' They went up a narrow walled-in staircase with strips of wallpaper hanging off the wooden board walls. She opened a door.

'Heavens!' said Lucy. 'A telephone!'

It was a very ancient black phone, the sort with the little drawer in the bottom that pulled out to give you phone numbers.

'Feller that had the shop afore Liz lived up here, no, I tell a lie, the feller afore him. He was a jeweller, so he had to live over the shop, for the burglars. Must have been his.' She picked up the phone and held it to her ear hopefully. 'Dead. Cut off. Not much call for phones round here. Liz never used it.'

They went from room to room. The rooms were big; at least, two of them were; the third was a windowless black box of a bathroom. There were brown stains on the ceilings, like maps of unknown continents. If the roof didn't leak now, it had in the past.

'Liz made old Bartlett have the roof done, afore she took the shop. At least, he let her off the first month's rent, on condition she had it done herself. It's sound enough. Liz knew what she was doing. Goin' to have it, then?'

There was no doubt in Lucy's heart. This place was *meant* to be. A gift from the gods, who had finally relented. With a phone number to give Daddy in the *Telegraph*. She rubbed away the dust from the centre of the dial; the dust of years.

Thraleby 1545.

'In loving memory of Nathaniel Thraleby, died the first of

49

May 1945. Still sadly missed by Rachel Kingsmith and family.'

Daddy seemed suddenly achingly near. As if she only had to pick up the dead phone to hear his voice. The room swam warmly round her. But she made herself say grudgingly, 'I'll give it a try for three months.'

Chapter Seven

Lucy spent the rest of that day in violent motion. Back to the hotel, to ring up British Telecom, the Electricity Board, even the local council about dust-bins. She used the phone in the lobby, because it had all the telephone directories handy, and she stood there saying loudly, over and over, 'My name is Rachel Kingsmith and I've taken over the antique-shop at seven, Barnston Road, Thraleby . . .'

Ears flapped all over the place; let them flap. They were helping her to create herself. The more she said 'Rachel Kingsmith', the more she felt like Rachel Kingsmith. By lunchtime she felt sufficiently Rachel Kingsmith to change into jeans and a floppy sweater, and went off to clean her new premises. The shop itself wasn't too bad. The departed Liz had papered it with pink roses, and fitted white Formica shelves along two walls; the floor was nice red quarry-tiles. Liz had done out the kitchen, too. It was all just dusty . . .

'Hereyar, love.' Her next-door neighbour was back, brandishing a huge and ragged broom. 'Since we're going to be neighbours you'd better call me June. June Hattersley. Everyone knows me round here.'

Again, Lucy was amazed at the difference between the face and the voice. Dress June up, and she wouldn't look out of place at a London first-night, with that slim elegant figure.

Until she opened her mouth. When she quacked like a duck. How had those exquisite genes got into this sad valley?

Some wandering American airman from Burtonwood Base, after the war? Some lonely foreign aristocrat, having a one-night stand with a pub-owner's daughter?

'I'm going down Big Artie's this afternoon,' said June, lighting up another half-smoked fag and leaning against the doorpost to support her coughing. 'He's just done a house-clearance. I'll introduce you if you like. He'll go stubborn on you, else; he can't stand toffs. But he'll be OK if he knows you're a friend of mine. He gets some good stuff sometimes, after a death.'

After she'd brushed out the shop, Lucy went down to the local mini-market for Cardinal floor-polish and dusters. The windows of the mini-market were boarded up with huge sheets of rain-stained plywood. People had stuck posters on them, advertising concerts for pop-groups she had never heard of, like 'Poisoned Electrick Head'. Other people had whiled away the time tearing strips off them. But even that was better than the red aerosolled graffiti.

GO HOME PAKKY BASTARD.
BENAZIR TAKES CREDIT CARDS.

She gave a very thin smile. She'd certainly obeyed Daddy's instructions. Who'd think of looking for her here?

She liked the couple who ran the mini-market. A Pakistani woman who said nothing, but gave her a shy warm smile as she took her money. And the husband, who insisted on shaking her by the hand, and wishing her all the best with her new shop.

'Maybe the village is looking up, when gracious ladies like you come.'

News certainly travelled fast.

*

52

'We'd better take my estate car,' said June after lunch. 'You might see something large you like. Big Artie offers to deliver. He only tells you he's charging you God knows how much afterwards, mingy sod.'

June's car was an old green Morris Minor shooting-brake, with lacy skirts of rust, and moss growing on the wooden windowsills.

'You'll have to get in my side, love. Your door's tied with wire.'

The car started finally; after a symphony of whines and clicks that reduced Lucy to despair, there was a tremendous bang from the rear end, and a cloud of oily smoke.

'Hang on,' said June, 'and brace your legs. That seat's coming loose from the floor.'

And they were off.

Big Artie had a shop in Easton, the next little town down the valley. Or rather, he had an Emporium. It said so, in garish gold letters two feet high, on a long sagging sheet of puce hardboard.

BIG ARTIE'S EMPORIUM. HOUSES CLEARED.
ANYTHING OLD BOUGHT.

'I've offered him *me* twice,' said June, 'but he says I'm a modern repro. He likes a laugh – sometimes it makes him drop his prices.'

Big Artie was big indeed. He was wearing khaki shorts and his hairy legs, all big muscles and big boots, stuck from under his desk. His big bare hairy arms lay on the desk-top, and they were not so much tattooed as a living book.

DEATH BEFORE DISHONOUR. With a skull and crossbones.

MOTHER. Enclosed inside a coiled cobra.

TWO PARA FOREVER. With the regimental wings. That was all Lucy had time to read, before Artie looked up, squinting his eyes against the light from the doorway, and said, 'What you two tarts want?'

'Just done a house-clearance have ya?' asked June.

'Nothing worth looking at. All just old rubbish.'

'We like old rubbish,' said June, pushing past him.

'Aye, well, rubbish likes rubbish. You'll not find anything.'

'Take no notice,' whispered June. 'Flora must've upset him again. She buys stuff off him, then comes back and boasts how much profit she made on it. It puts him in a bad mood for days, then you can't get a bargain for love nor money.'

Not that a bargain seemed likely; it was not so much a shop, thought Lucy, as a casualty-clearing station for wrecked and disembowelled lives. Stacks of stained pink mattresses; a table lamp in the form of a blue plastic bunny; a frog made of sea-shells varnished to look like toffee, a flesh-pink artificial leg cut off above the knee; towers of broken 78 rpm gramophone records, four 'Presents from Majorca' and a mirror with fiddly corners and flowers painted wildly all over it in household paint.

And then, quite suddenly, a clock on the wall. A big Ansonia, like they'd had at home. Marked fifty pounds. And Daddy had paid a hundred and fifty for his. Lucy's stomach contracted with that old hunter's excitement.

June noticed her interest. 'Does it go?' she shouted to Big Artie.

'Aye, if you push the pendulum. About twice a minute.'

His joke came out so bad-temperedly that neither of them laughed at it.

Lucy looked at the pendulum. 'He's not hung it properly,' she whispered.

'Try and get it going,' whispered June. 'I'll distract him. He doesn't know a thing about clocks. Silly beggar *boasts*

54

about it.' She drifted back to Big Artie saying, 'You seen Flora recently?'

A rumble of menacing thunder emerged from Big Artie, and rolled on and on. Leaning over two chipped and food-splattered baby's high-chairs, Lucy unhooked the pendulum, hung it back correctly, and gave it a push.

Softly, beneath the rumble of Big Artie's voice, she heard it ticking. Then it went off-beat, like a limping man. Then stopped. Lucy checked the angle it hung on the wall. It was cockeyed. She straightened the clock. It started a steady beat. There was nothing wrong with it.

'You can't get it going then?' asked June, coming back with a wink, and shoving the clock wildly askew again. She bellowed, 'Artie, what's the best price you can do my friend? She'll have to take it to the clockmakers and that'll cost her plenty.'

'Fifty – what I've marked on the label. I've got a chap interested – he's coming back tomorrow.'

'That's what you always say,' shouted June. 'Forty?'

'Forty-five. You tarts would steal the coat off me back.'

'Forty-three. In notes!'

'Pay the wife!' He nodded his head towards the far corner of the shop, where a plump, very respectable-looking middle-aged lady in a white blouse was sitting knitting by a struggling coal fire.

There were other things – two nice kitchen chairs with turned legs, obviously a pair, though one was painted bright pink and the other stripped and varnished. A small roll-top desk, with a row of fag-burns along the top. In the end, after a lot more insults had been exchanged between Artie and June, Lucy got the lot for a hundred and ninety-five pounds. As she paid, June said, 'Crumple every note as you pay, love. Make sure you haven't got two stuck together.'

As they were loading up outside, Lucy heard Artie's wife call, 'Give me a hand, Artie. I need to go upstairs.'

Lucy saw her struggle to rise; saw the crippled leg, the heavy irons, the walking stick. Saw the look on Artie's face, as he helped his wife through the cluttered shop. The smile, the gentleness . . .

'Aye,' said June at her shoulder. 'He dotes on her. She was crippled when he married her. He's made her a wonderful husband – they've got two kids at school.' She raised her voice. 'Tara, Artie!'

'Told you I had nowt,' shouted Artie, as he vanished upstairs with his wife.

'Heart of gold,' said June. 'Heart of gold.'

Lucy lay in her hotel bed that night, and listened to the sounds around her, the tiny creaks as a member of the night-staff passed on some mysterious quest up the corridor, and thought of the shop and curled her toes with pleasure. The shop was a tiny candle in a dark and terrifying world. A tiny candle of normality where the ordinary things still mattered, buying and selling and paying the rent and the clutch on June's car starting to go.

Daddy had said trust no one, but she trusted June with all her heart. One look at that face was enough. June was lonely, and made no secret of it.

'It'll be nice to have someone to talk to, about women's things. Not just beer and football. I always wanted a daughter, but I got nowt but three lads an' a miscarriage. You get sick of men, don't you?'

And of *course* June liked a profit; she counted notes as if she was going to eat them. But what harm was there in that? Lucy needed stuff, and June had it, and could find it. June could teach her a lot. With June, a future was possible . . .

So when the dark clouds of fear began to invade her mind again, Daddy and MI5 and . . . she clung to the shop and June as if they were the only candle in the world.

Still thinking of June and the shop, she fell asleep.

Chapter Eight

Lucy pulled the chain of the outdoor loo with deep satisfaction and re-fastened the big padlock on the loo door. She stared at the wall of the back yard in satisfaction too; blackened stone nearly seven feet high, with broken glass set in old concrete on the top. At the stout yard gate, also newly padlocked. Nothing in the gracious house at home had ever pleased her half so much. This was Lucy's castle. Before, home had just been somewhere you lived; here, it was something you *made*.

What a mad week it had been! A week of sweeping, dusting and slapping on paint. Only the tide of new paint drove back her fears. If thought became unbearable, undercoat another door. But the old shop fed her too; every sooty stone of it; the bedraggled sparrows that came for the crumbs of her pies and pasties in the back yard; even the black-beetles that scurried for sudden refuge under the kitchen sink. They were a hundred times more real than the hotel had ever been. And with everything she did, this real world grew, and pushed back the unreal world of her fears. She said, let there be light, and the electricity board turned on the power, so she could use her new kettle to make a first cup of coffee for June. She turned the single cold-water tap, and the water flowed. Only British Telecom were slow to come to her beck and call, as BT linemen dug a hole fifty yards up the village street, and exposed wires in the bowels of the earth.

Once the electricity was on, she worked late, till she was ready to drop. Got fish and chips at the late-night chip-shop on the way back to the hotel, and ate them in the car, sitting in the dark watching people pass laughing and quarrelling and kicking tin cans, unaware that she was there. That strengthened her too, made her feel a furtive creature of grim concealment, of the dark; a spy. Once back in the hotel, she went straight to her room, with only a curt nod to the night porter, and straight to bed.

Every muscle in her body ached, and she was glad of it; her aches were more real than her fears, as she scanned the late news on the telly from bed, just checking there was no news of Daddy. Then she slept the sleep of total exhaustion, without dreams.

At the shop the bedroom ceilings were shining white now; the continents of damp-marks gone. The walls were pale green and primrose, the staircase white. The old kitchen range shone with 'Zebrite'. So many tiny triumphs . . .

There was a banging of knuckles on the shop door. June waving and grinning excitedly, clutching a large Heinz Baked Bean box against her frail chest with her other hand. A cat's head poked out the top. Two kitten heads.

'June, they're lovely, but I'm not sure . . .'

'It's you or drowning, love. He's going to drown them tonight for certain . . .'

Lucy looked at the friendly furry faces. Saw them crumpled and sodden in death, droop-eyed and open-mouthed. A mixture of warmth and fury rose in her. The water would not have them. They would be the garrison of her castle . . .

Quite oblivious of their narrow escape, the three cats sniffed into every corner, rubbed their fat furry cheeks against chair legs and Lucy's legs alike; then had a fine time chasing up and down stairs.

'Patel keeps the cheapest cat food,' said June, and left her with her new family.

Another crazy impulse made her fetch the pile of rubbish from her spring-cleaning: newspapers, an old broken seed-box, odd chair legs, and pile them into the grate of the kitchen range. Her match sparked into life, the paper caught, shadows danced on the walls of the dark afternoon. The cats gathered to stare at the thin dying blaze with dreaming eyes, and wash themselves, and suddenly it was a sort of magic. The departed, those who had once lived in the shop, seemed to return like the cats, and bless her. The house became a home again, and not all the powers in Whitehall could prevent it.

When the fire had finally died, she made up her mind and picked up her car keys, and drove back to Big Artie's. Big Artie had beds . . .

But Big Artie wasn't there. Only his missus, knitting, knitting.

'How many beds?' she asked, comfortably, as if it was the most natural thing in the world.

And for some reason Lucy said, 'Two,' and added, 'singles'. It all came to her in a flash. She had a kitchen to sit in, in the evenings; the room with the phone would be her bedroom, the primrose room. And the green room should be for Daddy, which was the craziest thing of all. But suddenly she made up her mind that some day he would come there, if it took till the end of the world. Some day he would come there, and sink down weary on the bed, and then she would make him happy again.

'Setting up house, are yer?' said the woman. 'That's our main business, setting up houses for young girls. For the Social Services. Young girl gets pregnant, Social Services and Social Security have to house her – give her a council house. Artie can set them up a house for four hundred pound . . . Just the basics, mind, but we try to do it as nice as we can. There's a whole housing estate, full of young girls with babies, up Frampton. It's their way of getting freedom, see? A girl used to get free by starting her first job an' paying her mum rent. But now there's no jobs, they get free of their family by getting themselves pregnant . . .' She glanced, in a motherly way, at Lucy's waistline, making Lucy suddenly want to suck her stomach in.

'S'alright,' said the woman, in a friendly voice. 'I can see you're not in the pudding-club.' She struggled to her feet with great difficulty, and led Lucy into other rooms at the back of the shop she hadn't seen before. 'We've got some lovely curtains . . . nearly new. And you'll want a little cooker, electric. They don't have gas up your way. Electric's less bother anyway.' And she thought of things that Lucy wouldn't have thought of, like rugs and bedside cabinets. All her stuff was scratched and looked a bit washed-out and weary, as she did herself, but Lucy could see it was clean.

'Artie'll deliver tonight, when he gets home. After dark . . . we don't want folks being nosy, do we?'

Lucy darted her a look of horrified suspicion; but the lady was placidly adding up sums in pencil, on the margin of that morning's copy of *Today*. 'Folks is *so* nosy round here. You don't want them seeing all you've got . . .'

The shadows of MI5 dissolved, in Lucy's mind, into visions of old women in curlers, peering round the edge of their curtains. There was no possible link between old women and MI5, was there? She tried a breathy laugh, to brush away the idea. And yet eyes were eyes, and there were eyes everywhere . . . better Big Artie after dark than a furniture van in daylight, with the name of a big store on the side.

'That's two hundred and twenty pounds fifty-five, love. I'll knock off the fifty-five for luck. No charge for delivery.

61

Tell Artie I said that.' From the set of her lips, Lucy could tell that Artie didn't get all his own way.

Artie had come after dark. He'd knocked quietly as if he was in some plot. He had a silent youth with him, whom he didn't bother to introduce. In fact, Artie was very quiet and shy altogether. Quite a different, respectful Artie. Where did she want this putting? Where did she want that?

She had one embarrassing moment, when he saw the Ansonia clock on the wall, ticking away.

'You got it going, then?'

'Yes . . . yes,' she said, suddenly ashamed at the trick she and June had played on him, and him with a crippled wife.

'That's all right, love,' he had said gently, awkwardly. 'I know I don't know nowt about antiques. I don't pretend I do, like some. All this yak about Chippendale and Art Noove. A chair's just a chair to me. I don't mind them making money out o' me, providing they don't come back and swank about it, after. I left school at fourteen . . .'

'I think you do a very good service,' said Lucy stoutly.

His face cracked into a shy grin. 'S'a living. Just! D'you want more clocks? I'll keep me eyes open for you. Give you a ring. Anything else you want?'

'Chairs, any nice polished chairs. Little tables, but no fag-burns. Anything old, really, that's nice.'

'Right. I know you won't try and diddle me, like some.'

And of course that made it impossible ever to diddle him again.

As she watched his tail-lights dwindle away, she thought maybe that was the way he'd planned it.

*

'You're not thinking of *living* here?' said June, two days later.

'How do you know that?'

'You've got curtains up . . .'

'Hotels cost the earth,' said Lucy defensively. 'And there's the cats . . .'

'Nobody's lived over these shops for years,' said June. 'Old Bartlett won't like it, but I suppose he'll have to lump it.'

'Does he have to know?'

'You don't know village gossip, love. But a young girl like you, living on her own down here! I wouldn't live down here, even if I had a Dobe and a sawn-off shotgun. The young drunks at weekends . . .'

'Well, I'm going to,' said Lucy. 'In London, girls my age are living in Docklands. And in New York . . .'

'Yuppies,' said June. 'I didn't mind being a Hippy – I was at the Isle of Wight, the last time Jimi Hendrix played, but damn being a Yuppie. Me frame wouldn't stand it. Have you had the Yuppie flu yet?'

'No, and I don't intend getting it. Even if I do live down here.'

'You'd better go and see Trev. He does shutters. Don't try and ring him up. He's always either out on a job or in his workshop and he can't hear the phone.'

She found Trev's house with little difficulty; there was a pick-up truck outside, painted thickly in purple, with 'TREV' across the tailgate in big white lettering. It had huge home-made bumpers, in three-inch steel tubes, welded on the front and back, and an equally huge roll-bar behind the cab. No less than three tall radio-aerials stuck up from the cab.

She knocked, timidly. Then she knocked very loudly. Then she thumped on the door with her fist.

The door opened immediately.

'I heard you the first time,' said a very polite voice.

'June sent me. I need window-shutters.'

'Come in.'

It wasn't that easy. A full-sized stuffed grizzly bear stood in the middle of the hall, holding an elderly black gent's bicycle in one paw.

'That's Fred. Fred Bear. He's a bit fredbare in places.'

She followed him into some inner sanctum, in which the walls seemed papered with ticking wall-clocks. He turned to face her.

He was wearing a wide-brimmed trilby hat that was pure 1930s. And even though it was summer, he wore a long dark belted overcoat. And a black beard grew round his chin from ear to ear, and he wore little old gold-rimmed spectacles.

But the weirdest thing was that, just behind him, hugely enlarged, was a photograph she knew. A photograph of the first Communist revolutionaries in some Paris street. Lenin, Trotsky, Zinoviev, staring at her with spectacled, fearsome righteousness. And behind them, in his broad-brimmed trilby hat and beard . . . Trev. It was him . . . it *had* to be him. She stared from the real face to the coarse-grained black-and-white photograph face. Same snub nose, same straight eyebrows.

'Trick photograph,' said Trev. 'I stuck myself over Kamenev and enlarged it. The camera cannot lie . . .' He laughed, rather wickedly.

'Shutters,' said Lucy, feeling a bit faint.

'I can't do them for you before next Wednesday. We're busy at Social Security at the moment. But next Wednesday afternoon, I have a half-day . . .'

'Do you work for Social Security?' she asked in amazement, staring at his gear.

'Yes, why?'

She could think of no polite answer.

'D'you think all this is mad?' he asked, waving an arm at the clocks, the chairs, the beautifully polished models of battleships over the fireplace, so many things packed so close there was no way to pass between them. 'This is what keeps me sane. It's working for Social Security that drives me mad. Telling mothers they're entitled to two-thirds of a baby's cot, when they haven't even got a loaf of bread in the house. This is *sane*.'

'Are you married?' she gasped. She couldn't help it slipping out.

'Course I'm not married,' he said crossly. 'Working for Social Security all day, and doing antiques half the night. When would I find time to be married?' He led her through the small old house. 'D'you think any woman could stand this?' Small clocks even lined each side of the stair-treads. 'It would drive any normal woman mad.'

'Perhaps you should try an abnormal woman.'

'Tried those. Doesn't work. Even they start tidying and dusting.'

'But . . . don't you ever want . . . children?' He must be nearly thirty.

'These *are* my children. See those three wall-clocks there? Found them on a bonfire that hadn't been lit yet. Mate of mine got the job of clearing a primary school they were going to demolish. I asked whether I could look round first. There were these three clocks . . . glass smashed, pendulums gone, spattered with cement and paint . . . but I got them for ten quid, and now they live again. People just don't know what to do with stuff, so they smash it and burn it, put

65

it in dust-bins. Stupid. You've heard of the Save the Children Fund – well I'm the Save the Clocks Fund.'

'D'you ever sell any?'

He glared at her with a dark angry suspicion that quite equalled Trotsky's in the photograph.

'Would you sell your own children?' Then his face softened. 'We'll see, we'll see. Now what about these shutters?'

On the way out, she saw a beautifully lettered shop-sign for a florist's.

'Do you do sign-writing as well?'

'A bit. What do you want?'

He was as good as his word. By the Wednesday evening, the shutters were in place; silvery wire grids that you hooked over at the top, and padlocked at the bottom. He showed her how to put them on. And above them, very grand in gold on green, in Roman lettering:

RACHEL KINGSMITH ANTIQUES

She paid him, and as he turned to go, he bent and picked something crumpled from behind her door.

'You've got a letter.'

It was a bill for reconnection from British Telecom.

How dare they charge her, before they'd done the work?

She ran upstairs, and lifted the old black phone on the bedside table in what was now her bedroom.

The dialling tone came down her ear out of the black earpiece, turning her cold with a sudden fear.

The time had come.

*

God, it was so *complicated*.

She had the notice about Nathaniel Thraleby written out. That was the easy part. Only she mustn't write it; she must *print* it. The *Telegraph* might keep it, file it, where police eyes might see it later.

Handwriting was evidence . . .

And there would have to be a covering letter, otherwise it wouldn't look right. But she couldn't *print* a covering letter – that would rouse the *Telegraph*'s suspicions. Make them think it was a hoax. They wouldn't print a hoax, and then all chance of contact with Daddy would be lost . . .

The first insuperable wall loomed before her. She began to panic.

Typewriter, fool. Typewriter. Buy a typewriter. A cheap one, in W H Smith's.

But every typewriter was different. The police could turn typewriters into evidence . . . the police experts. A vision of a courtroom rose before her . . . the judge . . . God! Lucy Rachel King Smith you are accused . . .

Dump the typewriter into the river immediately afterwards. *Which* river? The rivers round here weren't deep enough. Somebody would find it. A canal in Manchester . . . suppose somebody saw her dumping it? Fool, people dropped things into Manchester canals all the time.

And how would she pay the *Telegraph*? She didn't dare write a cheque. Enclosing a twenty-pound note in the letter would look suspicious . . . Postal order!

But didn't postal orders carry the stamp of the post office who issued them? And there would be a postmark on the letter. She would have to buy the postal order and post the letter hundreds of miles away . . . Manchester was too near . . . down the M6 to the Potteries . . . the Potteries was a different world. But that would take half a day . . . June would notice her absence. June would ask where she had been . . .

Have a headache. No, that wouldn't do. June would knock on the shop door . . .

Oh, God, just tell June you were going into Manchester shopping. What's it got to do with June where you go shopping? Lucy Smith, you are turning into a total neurotic.

If you get into this shaking heap about posting a letter to the *Telegraph* how are you going to cope later on? If things *really* get rough?

Well, she had it all worked out now. She had spotted all the snags in time. Or had she?

No. Fingerprints on the letter, the postal order, the envelope . . . Could they get fingerprints off paper? She didn't know what they could do. Best not chance it. Buy a pair of thin summer gloves . . .

Would thin summer gloves be thick enough . . . ?

Buy winter gloves. Should she throw *those* away afterwards?

Then her sense of humour caught up with her. The idea of herself solemnly typing a letter wearing thick winter gloves, in high summer. She giggled, a little wildly.

It was time for the late news. Still shaking, she walked across and switched on the brand-new portable telly she'd bought for her bedroom at the shop.

God, she hadn't got a licence for that telly yet. And the shopkeeper who'd sold it to her had to inform the authorities she'd bought one. The last thing she wanted was TV vans snooping round here. She'd get one first thing in the morning.

The world was all traps . . .

Then the news announcer swam up into focus, and her mind was still and watching, though her hands shook slightly.

There was still no news of Daddy on telly.

68

Chapter Nine

June stuck her head round the shop door. 'Have a nice shop in Manchester? Did you buy anything?' Her eyes were avid for the sight of luxury.

'Blouse and a skirt,' said Lucy, carefully offhand. She'd bought them specially for June's benefit, in Stoke-on-Trent. After she posted the letter to the *Telegraph* . . . The skirt was Jaeger, and the blouse silk and boy had they been expensive! But she had to keep up June's image of her. 'Want to see them?'

'Not now,' said June, with a self-denying pout. 'We'd better get on to the saleroom. Best get there nice an' early. Get a good seat, and plenty of time to nose around.'

They went in her shooting-brake.

'Funny place to hold an antiques auction,' said Lucy. 'In a cattle-market.'

'One day a month they clean the cow-muck off their wellies and pretend they're Sotheby's.'

They drove into the cattle-market across ribbed concrete roads, spattered with flattened cow-manure. Past endless empty cattle-pens and large notices advertising BOCM cattle-foods and Alfa-Laval milking machines. Parked by a long low battered wooden building with a verandah, which reminded Lucy vaguely of a Wild West saloon.

'I'll say one thing for them,' said June. 'They keep their overheads low. You're not paying for any fitted carpets . . .'

They got large cardboard numbers from the girl at the desk, and Lucy bought a catalogue for a pound.

'We can share, can't we?' asked June. 'Let's grab seats here. Close enough so the auctioneer can't ignore you, but to the side so you can see who's bidding against you. No, don't leave your catalogue to mark your seat. Some bastard will pinch it, and another bastard will pinch your seat. I'll leave my stuff. It's not worth pinching.'

Around one chair she draped her washed-out pale blue anorak, and on the chair next door she placed her straw basket, one handle mended with string, which held a very battered children's thermos flask covered with Little Noddies, and a large and greasy pack of sandwiches.

'Right, let's go for a nosy!'

The long low room was dark, and already full of cigarette smoke, and it seemed to Lucy a tangled jungle full of men in velvet jackets, men in cloth caps and Barbours, and women studiously chewing pencils. Over their shoulders, massive as policemen, peered six huge grandfather clocks, all telling a different time and all stopped. Rows of tables, sideboards and chests of drawers cut the whole room into little narrow streets, half of which appeared to be cul-de-sacs, which were causing a lot of excuse-mes, squeezings past and raising of caps. There were oil-paintings all over the walls, mainly gloomy and lifeless portraits of cows, pigs and sheep, hung four deep and at very peculiar angles. And on the tops of the tables and sideboards was an endless clutter of oil-lamps, Toby-jugs, sheep-shears and even whaleboned corsets. Lucy could see everything was tagged with a little number, but where to start? A sense of hopelessness overwhelmed her.

'What . . . ?'

'See that feller in the long brown coat and cap?' said June. 'Go and ask him a lot of questions. How much he

70

reckons things will fetch? Act helpless. Keep him talking as long as you can. Keep him busy.'

Baffled, Lucy did as she was told. She learnt the possible price of a fox-fur with suspicious yellow eyes in a dried-out fox's face; a pair of drunkenly leaning brass candlesticks and the largest of the grandfather clocks . . . What the hell was June up to?

The man in the brown coat suddenly stopped talking to Lucy in mid-sentence and bellowed, 'PLEASE DO NOT HANDLE THE GOODS, MADAM!' to someone over her right shoulder. She turned in time to see June put down a Toby-jug, and scamper off under a table like a shot rabbit.

'Damn the woman,' said the man to Lucy. 'What were you asking me again, madam?'

'What is meant by a Liverpool clock?' asked Lucy meekly. And that was how it went on for nearly an hour. June had her fingers into everything, and her head inside half of them. Twice the man threatened to throw her out altogether, but June just waved Lucy's catalogue in his face and said, 'I've paid me pound. You can't stop me.'

'I'd pay ten pounds to have you sod off!'

Finally, the auctioneer tapped his microphone and asked them to take their seats.

'A right load of old tat,' said June loudly; getting a nasty look from the auctioneer.

'You don't seem too popular round here,' said Lucy.

'You mean, handling all the stuff?'

'Perhaps they're frightened you'll drop it.'

'Frightened I'll find out where the cracks are, more likely,' said June indignantly. 'Never dropped a thing in me life. Couldn't afford to. How much you got to spend?'

'Two thousand.' Lucy had been to a building society in Stoke-on-Trent.

'In *notes*? Put your feet on your handbag, then. And don't bid more than *this* for anything.' June dumped Lucy's catalogue back in her lap. In amazement, Lucy saw neat prices Biroed in against every one of the four hundred items.

'Hold on to your hats,' said June. 'Here we go!'

The first item was a copper warming-pan. As the porter held it high in the air, June said, 'See the way he's using both hands? The handle's loose and the lid-hinge is three-quarters broken and there's a hole in the bottom. That'll not fetch much.' Her voice was not loud, but her sibilant whisper carried. The brisk bidding around them faltered at thirty-eight pounds . . .

June raised her hand and got it for forty.

'But you said . . .' said Lucy.

'Our Tim can fix the handle and hinge, an' the hole's nothing.' June's whisper was really a whisper now.

Five items on, there was a large German mantel-clock, with a finely carved case.

'I like that,' said Lucy.

'Pity it ain't got no works,' said June. 'I turned it round an' looked inside. All that's inside is a few bits of Bakelite and a length of flex. Some fool converted it to electric back in the thirties an' it went wrong.'

The bidding on the clock climbed by tens to a hundred and fifty.

'Some poor sod's in for a shock,' said June. 'Why don't they look *inside* things?'

Ten lots on, there was a fine old rocking-chair.

'Pity the seat's full of woodworm underneath,' whispered June piercingly. 'The public's scared of woodworm.'

The bidding faltered at fifty-five and June got it for seventy. 'You can fill up woodworm-holes with dark tan boot-polish, and it doesn't show at all,' she added, *sotto voce*.

72

'I looked at that chair,' said Lucy. 'I never even *saw* the woodworm.'

'Got me little torch,' said June, slipping it out of her pocket. 'Need a strong torch in a place like this.'

The porter held up a bundle of brass stair-rods, with fancy fleur-de-lis ends. The bidding climbed rapidly to a hundred and ninety-five.

'I don't *believe* it,' said Lucy. 'You've marked them at thirty!'

'Two rich bitches in the front row. They know each other, they don't like each other, and they can see each other bidding. Silly cows.'

Several times Lucy tried bidding for things she liked. But the prices leapt away from her like a startled horse, going up a hundred pounds in ten seconds. She tore after them, bidding with spirit, waving her catalogue wildly in the air.

'You're not waving goodbye to somebody on a train,' said June. 'Just lift your hand. The auctioneer's got his eye on you.'

Then her hand would clamp like a vice on Lucy's knee. And Lucy would look down to see she'd exceeded the price June had Biroed in.

'It's like a madness, when you first start,' said June. 'You don't like being beat. Nobody likes being beat. It's worse than the drink and I should know. Our Tim's drunk every weekend.'

By one o'clock, all Lucy had managed was a set of oak butter-tubs, with gleaming brass bands. Still, she shouted out her cardboard number to the auctioneer with great pride.

'They'll sell well,' said June. 'People like them for putting plants in. It ruins them, but people buy them. I know the feller that ships them across from Ireland by the hundred.

Employs six men, just to polish them up. Gets them for a quid, an' sells them at twenty-five each.'

The first of the grandfather clocks came up, and hung at four hundred.

'I *want* that,' said Lucy. 'It will look good in the shop.'

'Have you measured your ceiling? That thing's nearly eight feet tall. People are frightened of them, they're so big. They don't sell.'

'I want it,' said Lucy, and got it for four hundred and fifty.

'I hope to God it works,' said June. 'Still, Trev'll always help you out . . .'

At the end of the auction, they paid at the desk, and drove round to the loading bay to pick up their stuff.

'What'll you do with these black whalebone corsets?' asked Lucy, handling them with some distaste.

'Oh, fellers buy them for a joke for their wives,' said June. 'You'll be surprised how many fools there are about . . . but it's all money.'

'And this dining-chair,' said Lucy. It was quite the ugliest chair she'd ever seen. Nobody but June had even bothered to bid for it, and she'd got it for a pound.

June laughed. 'Christmas is coming. An' that chair's *narrow*.'

'So . . .'

'Families coming for Christmas dinner . . . they're always a chair short . . . and a narrow chair fits in that much easier. I'll get four quid for that, come Christmas . . .'

Lucy shook her head ruefully. There was a lot more to the antique trade than she'd ever thought.

'All I've got is butter-tubs and a clock . . .'

'You're too much of a lady, lovey. You're from down

south. These northern scrums take some getting used to. Still, I've got a nice set of little Victorian balloon-backs coming in tomorrow that you'll like. An' a tripod table . . .'

'June, you're a brick.'

'For twenty-five per cent profit, I'm anybody's brick.'

Why did June flinch away from gratitude, as if it was poison?

She drove down the valley to buy her *Telegraph*. She couldn't trust herself to buy one in the local newsagents, where the young man knew her, and was shyly starting to talk to her about the weather. He would notice some falseness in her voice . . . and her sudden change to the *Telegraph*.

But it was more than that. She was starting to love Thraleby, black and dirty though it was. She loved the lollipop lady from the village school, who always had a wave and a smile for her. The warmth of the Patels at the mini-market; even the village children who pressed their noses against her shop window and stared at her solemnly, as if she was some exotic creature in its cage at the zoo; and greatly daring, shouted through the glass to ask when she was opening shop. She did not want the terrible dark that was outside to come near Thraleby . . .

She missed her message the first time she looked. Skipped from 'Simpson' to 'West-Oram' somehow, and felt a sag of disappointment. And then it leapt out of the newsprint at her like a tiger.

> **In loving memory of Nathaniel Thraleby, died the first of May 1945. Still sadly missed by Rachel Kingsmith and family.**

It seemed so prominent. It seemed (she held the paper this way and that to catch the light better) even to be printed in a heavier typeface than the other 'In Memoriams'. And suppose somebody in Thraleby village *took* the *Telegraph* . . . *Somebody* was bound to. Wouldn't they think it odd?

Rubbish, Lucy. Don't think rubbish . . .

But she was for it now. The balloon was about to go up, as Daddy always used to say . . .

But suppose he missed the *Telegraph* by accident that day? Suppose he'd got weary and given up, with having to wait so long? How would she ever know?

The thoughts squirrelled round her head all the way back to her shop. And all the rest of the day, while she polished and dusted like a fury, to stay sane.

She sat long beside the roaring fire in the kitchen range that night. In the old rocker she'd bought from June, with her feet on the clippie rug she'd bought from June for a quid. With June's cats at her feet, purring.

The Pennine wind howled round the corner of the shop, and tootled in the chimney. A few drops of rain hissed among the coals, but it only made the room more snug. She clung desperately to the snugness of June's world. It was all the more snug because it *was* June's world, not her own. People came and went in it, and you liked or disliked them, but it didn't really matter. It was like coming to live in some soap-opera for a while, like living inside *Coronation Street* or *The Archers*.

Then, for a while, she sadly remembered Cambridge, her place at Girton waiting for her, to read Modern History. But all that was fainter than a dream now, fainter than a memory. That was another life, a life that had belonged to

Lucy Smith. Poor dear Lucy, always eager to please, terrified of giving offence. The good little girl, who always did what she was told. Helpless Lucy could never have made a place to live in, carried a wad of notes in her handbag fit to choke a horse, seen through the tricks people pulled to live . . . Lucy had never been very solid, and now she was a ghost too. Nowhere!

She deliberately tried to regret Cambridge, the lovely buildings, the fund of knowledge, the trips in punts up the Backs. But she found she couldn't summon up any tinge of regret at all. The things she had now were *real*. Her own house, her own shop, stone and mortar and slate. Her own cats, her own antiques, each lovingly polished and shining like the sun. June . . . this scarred valley.

She was oddly content, like a gambler who has sat down at the table, smiled or grimaced at his opponents, arranged his chips in piles and got his cards sorted.

The game was on, and she was content to be in it. And safe tonight from the windy dark.

She heard a faint noise upstairs. A faint ringing like an old-fashioned alarm-clock *almost* like an alarm-clock, except she hadn't got an alarm-clock, she told herself sleepily.

Then she realized it was the old-fashioned phone.

And only one person could be ringing. Only one person knew her number . . .

Daddy.

She flew up the stairs, before it could stop. Daddy, ringing all those miles through the cold and dark. Daddy, in trouble, needing her, and she being so slow and stupid. Daddy, Daddy . . .

She picked up the black phone, trembling.

'Daddy?'

'No, love, it's not your Daddy.' It was a strange female

voice, very broad Lancashire. A voice with a laugh, a teasing knowledgeable laugh, at the back of it. Who on earth could it be, who knew about Daddy?

'Who . . . who . . . is it?'

'It's *June*, silly . . .'

'I didn't recognize your voice, for a minute. I didn't know you knew my number.'

'I saw it, when you showed me your bedroom. I remembered it. I thought I'd give you a ring, to make sure you're all right. I keep thinking of you, sleeping down there on your own. I just said to our Jim, it's not right, a young lass like that, sleeping down there on her own. Are you all right? You sound all funny, breathless . . .'

'It's just the running upstairs. I'm out of breath. I'm fine, really, snug as a bug in a rug. With the cats on my knee.'

'Well, as long as you're all right. I'll go and get our Jim his supper. Is your dad all right? Not poorly or anything? You sounded scared out of your wits . . .'

'Yes, Daddy's fine. He'll be coming up to see my new shop, soon. When it's open.'

'I'll look forward to meeting him. Well goodnight, love, sleep tight. I'm just *coming*, Jim!' The last was a squawking shout.

'Goodnight.'

Lucy sat down on the chair, till her heart stopped thumping. What a mess she was! Getting into a panic, just because the phone rang. What good was she going to be to Daddy, when he really did need her, if she panicked like that?

Chapter Ten

She was stripping down a wooden chest of drawers in the back yard, when the phone upstairs went the next time. She dropped the scraper and ran upstairs like a rocket, feeling a dab of paint-stripper on her bare arm starting to burn her skin as she ran.

But it wasn't Daddy; she recognized the rough uneven voice as June's eldest, Sammy.

'Tell me mam the van won't start, so I can't do that plasterin' today.'

She slipped out to give June the message, only pausing to run the stripper-burn under the cold-water tap in her kitchen; it stopped hurting immediately, but left a small red mark.

June greeted the news with an expression like sucking a lemon. 'If it's not his bloody van, it's his bloody back. He was on the beer last night – that's the truth. I don't know why I didn't drown the lot of them at birth. Sorry they're bothering you, love. I should never have told them you were on the phone.'

As Lucy left June's shop, she looked into the window of her own shop, and felt a glow of pride. The stuff in the window was building up nicely, and all her four new table lamps were lit, casting a cosy glow over the newly polished furniture. It looked a real antique-shop – one she would have loved to go into herself as a customer. June had got her the table lamps.

'Cheaper than spotlights, love. And you can sell them if you get a good offer.' June had got her so much. She only had to want something out loud, and June had it for her in a couple of days. And the prices she asked were cheap, very cheap, at least by London standards . . . Pity they hadn't been able to get the grandfather clock to work, though it looked very grand, now she'd polished it.

She had put up a notice in the window in bold red felt-tip, saying, 'Opening shortly'.

As she opened her own door, she saw with a shock that there were two men in the back of the shop. Her heart shrank and seemed to miss a beat. But the next second she saw they couldn't possibly be policemen, even plain-clothes policemen. Their skins were ingrained with dirt, as if they'd never been clean. And one was just too old, and the other had a figure, spindle-shanked and pot-bellied, that no Chief Constable would ever have stood for. His pale unhealthy face and shock of uncombed hair . . . They were both dressed in grey, not real grey, but the washed-out grey of dust. Grey baggy flannel trousers, grey jumpers with raggy elbows, and unbuttoned waistcoats over the top of them.

And yet they filled the shop with a strange authority. They did not even bother to look up as she came in, but continued to search the place, tipping over tables to inspect underneath, turning chairs upside down, peering into the privacy of her kitchen, even tipping the cats off her own private rocker and rummaging among her pots and pans.

She just stood speechless. First speechless with fear, then speechless with amazement, then speechless with rage.

The men talked to each other in grunts.

'Woodworm in the leg . . .'

'Only 1920s stuff.'

'Nowt here worth looking at . . .'

Lucy took a deep breath and said, 'Excuse me, this shop's not open yet.'

The spindle-shanked one gave her a look out of sinisterly innocent, wide-open blue eyes.

'Don't mind us, love. We're trade.' They went on turning the place over.

'This table lamp's not bad,' said the old man, and unplugged it, wrapping the flex around it, and putting it on Lucy's desk.

'Put that lamp back,' said Lucy. 'It's not for sale.'

'Oh, c'mon, love,' said the old man. 'Don't give us a hard time.' Then he said, 'I think we'll take this rocker, Jack,' picking up Lucy's private chair, and letting the old woollen cushion fall off on the floor. 'Don't want the cushion, though.'

'Put that chair *back*!' yelled Lucy, trying to grab it off him, and not succeeding.

'Don't fret, love. We'll give you a fair price, won't we, Jack? You mustn't mind our little ways. We're *trade*.' He started to carry the chair off towards the shop door.

Quick as a flash, Lucy turned the shop door key and shoved it in her pocket.

'This is *my* shop,' she said. 'And I'm not selling you anything.'

They stopped, and gaped at her.

'You'll not make a living that way, love. Is this a shop or isn't it? Or is it a bloody museum?'

'Mebbe it *is* a museum, Jack. Everything's *polished* . . .'

'Nowt worth having anyway. Not worth our calling here again.'

'Even that grandfather clock wouldn't fetch a hundred. Too big.'

'*I* wouldn't give her a hundred for it.'

'I paid four hundred and fifty for that clock.' Traitorous tears pricked at Lucy's eyes.

'By God, you were done then, love. Robbed blind. Who robbed you blind, love?'

'Never you mind!' shouted Lucy. 'Get out of my shop or I'll call the police.'

'But you've locked us in! She's locked us in, Bob, then she tells us to get out or she'll call the police. You can't win with this one.'

There came a sharp tapping on the window. Lucy looked up, brushing away a mist of tears with a furious hand, to see June standing there. She had never been so glad to see anybody. She unlocked the door, expecting June to wade in to her defence.

But June just smiled at the men, and said, 'Cup of tea waiting for you, next door, lads, when you're ready.'

'Right,' said the pot-bellied one. Then he turned to Lucy and said, 'We'll be back, after.' And they shambled off in the wake of June. Trembling still, Lucy returned her shop to some kind of order. By the time she'd finished, the two men were already carrying stuff out of June's shop to their battered blue Volkswagen van.

Finally, they came back with June into Lucy's shop. If they hadn't been with June, Lucy wouldn't have unlocked the door. This time they went for the smaller stuff; a trivet off the wall, an oleograph of grazing cows; a single candlestick; a silver-plated picture frame; saying grudgingly, 'What's the best price you can do me on this, love?'

Lucy, desperately trying to remember what she'd paid for the things, named prices off the top of her head. Finally, they had a heap of six objects.

'How much altogether, love?'

Lucy thanked God her school had taught mental arithmetic.

'Seventy-eight pounds.'

'That's seventy pounds to us, then. Ten per cent off for trade.' They began to pick up the things and head for the door.

'I've given you trade discount already!' screamed Lucy. 'I'm not giving you any more. Seventy-eight pounds or *nothing.*'

The men stared at her, and she stared back. Then they shoved the stuff back on the table, and silently walked out, leaving Lucy's heart pounding fit to burst.

They drove off, June waving to them as they went. Then June came back into the shop, dug a wad of greasy notes out of her long cardigan, and began sorting them out into fives and tens.

'They're not bad sorts really,' she said. 'A bit rough but . . .' She glanced at the abandoned stuff on the table.

'How much did you pay for that lot?'

'Fifty-two,' said Lucy, after looking through her book.

'So you could've sold it them for eighteen quid profit?' June looked incredulous.

'To *them*?' yelled Lucy.

'You mustn't mind their little ways,' said June. 'They do that to everybody. They're just trying you out. No point in bearing a grudge. Still, you quite impressed them . . .'

'How do you know?' asked Lucy in astonishment.

'They called you a hard-faced Yuppy bitch. From them that's quite a compliment. Don't worry – they'll be back.'

She returned to stripping the chest of drawers, after a quick cup of coffee. The paint-stripper had mixed with the old paint, then dried and set hard, like the toughest sort of toffee. She slapped on more paint-stripper viciously, managing to get a speck of it in her eye, on the rebound. She was still sloshing water into her eye, which was stinging like hell, when the phone went again.

'It's Sammy here. Will you tell me mam there's no milk left in the fridge?'

June just shrugged and said, 'Tell him to get on his bloody legs and walk down to the shop and buy some!'

Lucy went back to the phone and said, 'Get on your bloody legs and walk down to the shop and buy some.'

Sammy sighed heavily and hung up.

The paint-stripper had gone hard on the chest of drawers again. Lucy vowed that this would be the first and last time she would ever strip anything. When the shop bell went, she rushed through into the shop like an avenging fury.

But it was only Mr Patel from the mini-market and his wife, smiling gently. 'I have been admiring your beautiful shop and I have brought the missus to admire it too. If you will give permission! I know you are not open yet! But we are shopkeepers too. We know your problems.'

Lucy sat in her chair, and watched them going round, touching everything with gentle fingers, and sighs of admiration. June said that when people admired everything, you knew they weren't going to buy. They were paying you with admiration instead, because they felt guilty at wasting your time. But she found the Patels so soothing, after the English. They seemed to dance delicately from one object to another, and then they danced only between three objects, and then they were hovering over one, a Viennese wall-clock, touching it constantly and hovering from foot to foot, their voices rising in some sort of anxiety. Why had they grown so tense?

Then Mr Patel came back and stood over her.

'The missus likes your clock very much. It is like one her father had, back in Pakistan when she was a girl. Does it strike the hours, please?

84

Lucy went across, and pushed the hands forward, so it struck.

Mrs Patel sighed and clasped her hands together in ecstasy, and said something.

'She says it is exactly the same clock. It makes her feel like a young girl. It is our wedding anniversary soon . . .'

Lucy thought they were so sweet . . . then she realized they were staring at her with great, soft-eyed intensity.

'It is allowed to buy your clock?' asked Mr Patel gravely. 'Even though you are not yet open?'

'Yes,' she said stupidly. 'Of course.'

'You have the never-never?' asked Mr Patel. 'I will give you fifty pounds now, and every Friday night we will come and pay you ten more, and look at our clock.' He added anxiously, 'That is the price that is on? A hundred and twenty pounds?'

'I can let you have twelve pounds off – trade discount.'

They were so nice, she couldn't help saying it.

'Ah, but there is extra charge for never-never. You take twelve pounds off – I put twelve pounds on, for never-never. You are just starting out, and starting out is hard. One hundred and twenty pounds. Will you give me a receipt please?'

She looked up, into their shining soft brown eyes, full of unfathomable motives, and thought it was best to leave well alone, and wrote out her first receipt, for fifty pounds.

'On Friday, we will bring whole family to look at our clock! Goodbye. Good luck with your new venture!'

She sat on at her desk, feeling suddenly exhausted but acutely happy.

Then the phone went again, upstairs.

She picked it up and said, 'For God's sake, Sammy, what is it now? I'm trying to strip a bloody chest of drawers . . .'

There was a very un-Sammy-like silence, then a quiet voice said, 'Lucy?'

Her heart squeezed up so tight she couldn't breathe.

'Daddy?'

'The same, kitten. I got your message in the *Telegraph*. Where are you living?'

'Seven, Barnston Road, Thraleby, West Yorkshire. Daddy, I've got an antique-shop! I've set up my own antique-shop! And there's bags of room above the shop! You can come here when—'

'Wait!' he said, very sharply. Then continued, as if to himself, 'Seven Barnston Road. Seven Barnston Road.' She knew he was committing it to memory. He would never write it down.

When he seemed satisfied with himself, he said sharply, 'Are you still driving Mummy's car?'

'Of course not! Not for over a week!'

'Where have you left it?'

'Ringway Airport – long-stay car park.'

'Oh, you are a bright girl! I knew you'd have done something bright. The police haven't been on to me about it. Which is just as well – that could have been awkward. *Very* awkward.'

She glowed. 'I've got another car – it's a—'

'Don't tell me, kitten. I don't need to know. Have you got the money into building societies?'

'Of course.' Suddenly she felt a spurt of anger. Did he think she was a total fool?

'What's this about antiques, Lucy?'

She tried to tell him all about it again. But he cut her off short.

'I don't think that was very wise. The police will soon know about us and antiques . . .'

86

'It was all I could get. I looked and looked. You don't know how hard it is.'

'Lucy! Don't start getting het-up. I suppose you'd better stay, now you're settled. Make the best of a bad job. We don't want these antique people reporting your sudden disappearance . . .'

Oh, why was he being so *unfair*?

'Lucy? You still there?'

'Yes,' she said miserably.

'Sorry to snap. But I *don't* like this antique business. Still, as I said, we must make the best of it, now. Try not to make any more nonsenses, kitten . . .'

'How are you?' she said, wretchedly.

'So-so.' Which told her nothing. 'I won't ring you again during the day. I don't want you tied to the phone. I'll ring after seven in the evenings. That all right?'

'Yes.'

'Don't expect me to ring often. It looks suspicious, me ringing from call-boxes. OK?'

'OK.' She thought, Daddy, are you really all right? Daddy, do you love me? But she didn't say it. He sounded so cold, so distant. So . . . scared.

As if he suddenly read her thoughts, he said belatedly, 'I love you, kitten. Are you all right?'

'Yes,' she said, frozen. What else was there to say?

'Lots of people ringing up to enquire about you . . .'

'Who?' A freezing hand clutched her heart.

'Oh, just Claire, rather cross. And Karen, Sharon, Annie, they all sound the same to me. I told them you'd gone off on holiday to your Aunt Kate's.'

'Thanks.'

'Are you *sure* you're all right, kitten?'

'Yes.'

'You sound miserable . . .'

Oh, go away, Daddy. Get off the line for God's sake, and let me cry in peace . . .

'Must go, kitten,' he said hastily. He suddenly sounded . . . what? And then he was gone, and there was just the dialling tone. But before she could give way to any emotion, while she still sat clutching the black phone as if it were Daddy, June's 'Coo-ee! Anybody there?' came floating up the stairs.

She walked down slowly.

'You all right, love? You look like you seen a ghost!'

June's eyes were sympathetic, but very sharp.

'It's just the fumes from the stripping,' Lucy said, wiping her eyes, which were wetter than she liked.

'I saw you'd been at it. Nasty stuff. But you mustn't leave it to set hard like that. D'you want our Sammy to strip it for you? Only cost you a tenner. Give him something to do, the idle little sod.'

'Yes, please,' said Lucy.

'I'll take it up at lunchtime, when I go and get his dinner.'

Lucy wondered faintly whether it was good for idle little sods to have their dinners got for them.

She sat with her lunchtime Cornish pasty, crumbling it between her fingers. Why had Daddy rung off so suddenly? Were they closing in on him? Had they just arrested him? If they had, how would she ever find out? Daddy! Daddy!

But there was resentment in her as well. She had felt so strong and competent till he rang up, and now she felt so weak and helpless. Rachel Kingsmith was doing OK, but Lucy Smith . . . ? She suddenly had a traitorous desire not to be Lucy Smith any more. She wanted to be Rachel Kingsmith and to battle on with Rachel's life and be happy.

But that was a very dreadful thing to want! How could she be so selfish, when Daddy was in such trouble . . .

The light outside her shop window darkened abruptly, as if a cloud had come over the sun. A purple cloud, lettered TREV.

Trev helped. Because he didn't examine her face closely and tell her she looked as if she'd seen a ghost. In fact he didn't look at her at all. All his eyes were for the grandfather clock in the window.

'June said you couldn't get it going. I just hope the ropes aren't tangled . . . Oh, God, they are, all round the striking train. What've you done to it, it's like a rat's nest in here!' He had his head inside the clock, peering up. 'Hey, can you go and get my tool-kit from the pick-up? There's a small thin pair of pliers in it . . .'

As his voice echoed hollowly from the big mahogany case, she thanked heaven for the insensitivity of men.

Trev shoved a rolled-up *Exchange and Mart* under the left side of the grandfather, and swung the pendulum again, and stepped back.

'That sounds better. Beat's more even. Should keep going now. Nothing really wrong with it. A bit dirty but . . .'

'How much do I owe you?'

He turned and looked at her for the first time. His eyes were large and blue and merry. That's why he could never really look like Lenin or Trotsky, in spite of his glasses and trilby hat and beard. Lenin and Trotsky had narrowed eyes, like snakes. Except snakes didn't really narrow their eyes . . .

'For ten minutes' work? A cup of coffee?' He sat in her

89

armchair, and picked up Tibbie with a swift grab that Tibbie didn't seem to mind at all.

Trev seemed in no hurry to go. He just sat, playing with Tibbie's ears and taking an occasional sip of coffee, and relaying gossip about the trade. Big Artie and Flora, and someone called Jessie in the next valley, and Vera and Lesley, on the road back towards Manchester. He made the local antique trade sound like a little village, where everybody knew everybody.

'They're all looking forward to meeting our famous Yuppy . . .'

'Which Yuppy?'

'You,' said Trev.

'Me?' said Lucy. 'I'm not a Yuppy.'

'June says you are. Says you've got a great big shop down south . . .'

'We've got a shop,' lied Lucy. 'But not a big one.'

'Where is it?'

It was a bad moment. She almost said 'London', but that would have been too close to the truth. So she said 'Exeter' instead. She knew the antique-shops of Exeter well, from going round them on holidays. And Exeter was the furthest place off she knew . . .

'Whereabouts in Exeter?'

'That steep street leading up towards the cathedral.'

'Near Minions?'

'Bit further down . . .'

'What're you called?'

'Exeter Antiques.'

'Been there long?'

'Only a year. We were in a little village outside before that.'

'That explains it. Haven't done Exeter for a couple of years. The shops there are always going bust. You think you've found a good one, and the next time you go, it's gone. I'll look you up, the next time I'm down.'

'When'll that be?' Her heart was in her mouth.

'Dunno,' he said. 'When I feel like it. Not this year, anyway. Going to the Black Forest this year. Looking for clocks. Hey, do you know what June's Timmy's done now? Painted the wrong house pink. When he got there and knocked on the door, there was nobody in, so he just started painting it pink. Four hours later, the owner comes home, and it's the wrong house . . . Should've been next door.'

Lucy gave a sigh of relief. She was off the hook for the moment . . . Or was she?

'Y'know,' said Trev, 'you're funny. You're not like a Yuppy at all.'

'How d'you know what Yuppies are like? Have you met many?'

Trev grinned at her. 'No. Not really. Just what it says about them in the papers. Knowing the price of everything and the value of nothing. Always talking into car phones in their BMWs. Money, money, money. Whereas you're like . . .'

'What?'

'A little girl playing at keeping house. All this decorating, and living down in this weird hole, and pleased as punch with everything, even your outside loo . . .'

She felt suddenly sick. She didn't know what to say. Was it *so* obvious? But she had to say something. Stupidly she replied, 'My father . . .' and then didn't know how to go on.

'Ah,' said Trev, closing his eyes with bliss and grinning from ear to ear. 'I see it all. Let *me* tell *you*. The shop down south is really your father's, right?'

91

'Yes,' she said, shaking with terror.

'And he runs everything, really? You were no more than a glorified shop assistant? Right?'

'Right,' she said weakly.

'And then he had this idea about opening a northern branch, to buy up antiques cheap, and ship them down south. And he's so busy making money, he let you be in charge, for the first time in your life? Right?'

'Right.'

His smile grew even broader. 'I'm a genius. And I reckon he'll be up here, to see how you're getting on, any moment now? Right?'

'Right,' she said.

'Well,' he said, 'he'll want to see your shop fuller than it is at the moment, won't he? I mean, it will hardly make up a vanload, will it, as it is? You'd better get out and buy before he comes, hadn't you? Look, I'll draw you a map of the best places to go . . .'

And he sat and drew one there and then, bless him. A map even with the road numbers marked. Flora's shop and Jessie's and Vera and Lesley's. And Ken's and Tom's and Harry Brimble's.

Finally he looked up shrewdly. 'And don't go all dressed up like a Yuppy, or they'll not give you a good discount. Wear your oldest jeans . . . Ah, well, must be off. Back to the treadmill.'

'Thanks for the help.'

'All part of life's rich tapesty, as they say in books . . . Tara.'

And he was gone, leaving her gasping. She felt like an actress in a play, and other people kept writing the script. And yet Trev would help now; help to make her and Daddy real, with his new round of gossip as he went from shop to shop. She couldn't ask for a better cover-story for Daddy.

If he ever came . . .

Flora sat sedately in the middle of her dark little shop, like a well-fed spider in a web of brass, and jewellery in glass cases. Every dealer seemed to go in for something different. Flora seemed to have an inordinate love of pressed-brass plaques to hang on the wall. Brass galleons with bulging brass sails floated on brass tempestuous seas; thieves sat playing cards in brass thieves' kitchens; brass crinoline ladies, brass retriever dogs . . .

'I like me brass,' said Flora comfortably. 'Ever since I was a little girl, I've liked me brass. Gives you something to clean on wet days; cheers you up. I get through thirty tins of Brasso a year, here. And it's not cheap.'

'Yes,' said Lucy. She had her eye on an old miner's lamp. Brass. Polished to within an inch of its life.

'You been to Big Artie's?' asked Flora.

'Not today.'

'Quite right. He's got nowt as usual, ignorant beggar. How can a man deal in antiques, when he knows nowt? I try to educate him, but he just doesn't want to know. Takes a pride in his ignorance. Boasts about it. What can you do with a man like that?'

Lucy put back the miner's lamp. It was a modern repro.

'Haven't got much in at the moment,' said Flora. 'Had an Arab gentleman in yesterday. He took everything I had. Looted me something cruel. But what can you do, when they fancy what you've got and they've got the money to pay for it?'

Flora sighed, luxuriously as a concubine. 'Very good-looking chap he was, very dark eyes, and he was straight at me trivets like a dog at broth. I don't know what me husband's going to say, when he gets home at the weekend . . . The money's nice, while you're counting it. But them trivets were *irreplaceable*.'

Lucy moved over to a black marble clock with highly polished brass columns. 'Does it go?'

'Just needs winding, love, that's all.' But she made no attempt to wind it.

'Got the key?' asked Lucy. Flora looked annoyed, and scrabbled in the drawer of her desk. 'Think that's it – it's the only key I've got, any road.' She passed it over with bad grace. Lucy tried it in the clock.

The clock was fully wound already. Lucy rocked it gently; no sound came from it. Flora said, a marked dislike creeping into her voice, 'You a student, love? Get a lot of students in here, looking for Victorian jewellery. I don't mind them coming in one by one, but they come in fours or fives. Then three or four of them gather round you, distracting you, and the other one pockets something. I've complained to the college; I've had the police in, but there's nothing you can do about it.'

'No, I'm not a student. I'm a dealer. Taken the shop next to June's. Trev told me about you . . .'

'Oh, *you're* the one . . . You don't want to bother with that old clock, love, it's broken. I only keep it for the brasswork . . .'

Lucy turned to two highly coloured prints of Victorian battleships. Obviously genuine, if only from the slight fly-spotting. 'How much are these?'

'Oh, our Nev wouldn't part with those, love. They're his favourites. He only keeps them in the shop to look at . . .'

Baffled, Lucy turned to a row of totally bogus Stafford-shire figures.

'A gentleman from Lancashire usually has *them*, love. He comes every month. A lovely man . . . a retired major . . .' Flora's voice flowed on and on, like time's never-ending stream in the Armistice hymn. It drilled right through Lucy's head. She couldn't think; she could hardly see. Finally able to stand no more, she said 'thank you' and turned for the door. With a last regretful glance at the Victorian battleships . . .

'I can do them for fifty,' said Flora, rapidly. 'Seeing as it's you.'

'But what about Nev?'

'He'll have to lump it. What's the good of having an antique-shop if you don't move the stuff?'

Lucy sighed, rather dramatically. 'I'm afraid the price is beyond me.' She moved to the door; put her hand on the handle, opened it. Looked back at the battleships and sighed again.

'Forty-five then,' said Flora. 'Seeing as we've had a nice chat. I do like a nice cosy chat, don't you? Makes up for never having a holiday . . .'

'What – not ever?' asked Lucy sympathetically.

'Oh, we can *afford* one. It's just that we don't dare to leave Young Nev on his own at home. I know what he's like. He'd have all his little mates around for an all-night party. You just can't trust the young these days . . .'

It was another half-hour before Lucy was able to break free, and then she had to leave in mid-spate. Flora's hands kept starting to parcel up the battleships in brown paper, and then relaxing again, as she went into another tirade against youth in general and Young Nev in particular; whereupon the brown paper would fly open again. In the end Lucy had to grab the battleships bodily and leave the brown paper lying there.

*

She put out her bedside lamp and lay back with a sigh. Too tired even to read.

But she knew she'd done well. Besides Flora's battleships, she'd got a mahogany whatnot (with all the knobs intact) from Ken. And a pair of brass doorstops in the form of galloping hussars from Jessie, who was not much older than she was herself and nice, with freckles and long red hair. And an Art Nouveau hallstand from Vera and Lesley who lived together and held hands and wore their hair short and why not? And an ancient poss-stick from Harry Brimble, who only had one leg, but who could get about like any young 'un.

She was just dropping off to sleep when the phone rang, jolting her upright. It was nearly midnight by her alarm-clock.

'Thraleby 1545,' she said cautiously.

'Hello, Thraleby 1545!' The voice was warm, with laughter in it.

'Daddy?' If it was, this was a very different Daddy . . .

'The same, kitten. Were you asleep?'

'Not quite. Are you all right?' He sounded so unlike himself.

'Been to the theatre. Decided to walk home across Hampstead Heath. Called in at the Spaniards for a couple, just before closing time. If anyone's trailing me, they've had a very expensive evening. And a very exhausting one. And now they've lost me. Lots of nice dark clumps of bushes on the heath. Lots of lovers too. Very embarrassing for Special Branch or MI5 or whoever they are.' He laughed again; a much longer laugh than she was used to.

'Daddy, are you *drunk*?'

'I've been drinking. But I'm not drunk. Not so drunk I can't lose a pair of very large gentlemen with big flat feet.'

'*Are* you being followed?'

'Who knows, kitten, who knows?' Another over-long laugh.

'Be *careful*, Daddy!'

'I'm celebrating, kitten. I've got *reason* to celebrate. There's only one more bit of evidence I need, and then I've *nailed* the beggars. Though how I'm ever going to lay my hands on that last piece . . . Hey, kitten, I might be sending you a parcel. Keep it safe for me, till I need it, right?'

'Yes, of course.'

'The joke is, it'll be marked OHMS. I'm sending it via our own post-room. So they won't catch me carrying stuff out of the building, eh?'

'Daddy, *do* be careful!' Having him in this state terrified her.

'No more time now. Must go. Chap coming to use the phone-box. Big sort of bloke. Big sort of feet. Blasted heath – enter a copper. Bye, kitten. Take care!'

And he was gone.

She got little sleep that night, if any. The grandfather downstairs, so lovingly mended by Trev, clanged away the hours. Its tick might be soothing, but its strike was like the first ring of the phone. Yet the clock was the companion of her sleeplessness, not its cause.

Daddy. Drunk. She had never known him in the least bit drunk, even at Christmas when most people were a little; even Mummy. And the drink had let loose a different Daddy; younger, wilder, foolish even. Had there really been a policeman approaching his phone-box, or was it only Daddy's joke? Didn't he realize what a cruel joke it was, to play on her?

How well did she know him after all? Did the drink mean he was cracking up?

Her pillow was so sodden it scratched her face, before she realized it was no good crying. What was, was. Crying wouldn't change it.

The whine of the early milk float insisted it was a new day, and a day she had to get through. She sat up, on the edge of her bed, and finally faced the unthinkable thought. A world where Daddy was locked away; a world where she was on her own. For good.

She couldn't face it as Lucy, the tearful doormat. She could only face it as Rachel. Lucy must get smaller, be locked away somewhere safe. Rachel must get bigger, to look after her. Somehow, Rachel would cope.

She stood up and began putting on the armour of Rachel.

Chapter Eleven

'When you goin' to have yer opening?' asked June, leaning on her broom on the sunny morning pavement and grubbing in her anorak pocket for the inevitable half-fag.

'I suppose I'm open already,' said Lucy, a bit reluctantly. She didn't want to part with any of her highly polished treasures, leaving horrible gaps. And the shop was her strong refuge and her fortress and she didn't want the whole unknown world trampling through it, unstoppably.

'Oh, you'll have to have a *proper* opening,' said June. 'An official opening. With a drop to drink. They're all *expecting* it.'

'All?' asked Lucy weakly.

'All the dealers. An' all their best customers. Word gets round, you know. We could do wi' a bit of a do; cheer us up. And you might sell quite a bit. People who come feel obliged to buy, to give a good send-off. I thought next Saturday afternoon, about half-past three . . . I'll do some of those little vol-au-vent things, an' Flora's promised some sausage rolls an' Big Artie's wife does a grand apple pie. We can use paper plates to save the washing up, but we'll have to have glasses, about three dozen should do. I'll see the landlord of the Fletcher's Arms, he owes me a favour . . .'

'What do *I* do?' asked Lucy weakly again. She recognized a *fait accompli* when she saw one. Rachel would have to swim with the tide. If Daddy was sent to prison, these people were all she had.

99

'Dozen bottles of plonk, half white, half red. I'll get them for you. Mr Patel will give me ten per cent off, for trade.'

'How much?' said Lucy, her teeth on edge at the idea of *more* booze, more drunkenness. She felt in her handbag for her wad of greasy notes.

'Don't worry,' said June, sensing her reluctance and misunderstanding the reason. 'They'll all bring their own bottle anyway; all except those mean sods from Rochdale, who'll only come for a free skinful. You'll end up wi' more unopened bottles than you started with. Then you can sell them back to Mr Patel.'

On Saturday afternoon, Lucy lingered by the door of her little kitchen, an untouched glass of wine in her hand, and let June do all the socializing.

The shop was so full you couldn't see the antiques. The noise was deafening. She could hear Trev's voice booming through it.

'All part of life's rich tapestry.'

Harry Brimble had already demonstrated that a one-legged man really could do a tap-dance, to the chorused words of 'Tiptoe Through The Tulips' and a storm of applause.

Vera and Lesley were holding hands and cutting fellow-dealers to ribbons with their tongues. She heard Lesley say, 'And he said to this American, "Sir, that Westminster clock is genuine King George the Sixth," and the American said, "Gee, that's so *historical*," and gave him fifty pounds for it; twice what it was worth.'

June was hanging on to Trev, her arm right round him as if she owned him, really fancied him. And Trev didn't seem to mind at all.

'Oh, he's a lovely boy,' she said, 'a lovely boy. He sorted out me Davenport a treat.'

100

Further wild shrieks of laughter. A well-dressed, lost-looking man, who had just entered the shop, turned tail and fled. Lucy had a sad feeling he had been not only an outsider, but a potential customer . . .

And then a huge grey van drew up outside, darkening the window. A van as huge, grey and battered as a battleship after the Battle of Jutland.

A sudden hush fell. June muttered, 'God, who asked *him*?'

'He can smell the booze,' said Trev. 'Smell it miles away, like vultures smell rotting meat.'

Talk resumed, but less an uproar than an expectant buzz. It was obvious that everyone knew the man in the van. Who now got out, with a large wall-clock under his arm.

'Here we go!' muttered somebody.

The man came into the shop. He was tall and muscular, and shabby even by dealers' standards. His arms were bare and his sleeveless leather jerkin was scuffed, with tiny snags from top to bottom, as if he spent his whole life moving large sharp objects. The cropped blond hair on his head was nearly as short as the three-day growth of whiskers on his ruddy cheeks.

But it was his eyes that fascinated Lucy. Small and dark and far apart; totally expressionless, like the eyes of a great white shark. He looked around warily, as if expecting not to be welcome. Everybody was terribly busy talking to each other, yet watching the newcomer out of the corner of their eyes.

The man seemed to pick Lucy out. He came across to her and shook her hand with a palm that crackled with callouses like crumbling armour-plating. 'Congratulations on your opening. I've brought you a present to celebrate.' He indicated the clock, which had a battered walnut case and black dial with gold hands.

101

'For me?' stammered Lucy, suddenly terribly embarrassed. 'For nothing?'

'Norrexactly,' said the man. 'But cheap. Cheap to you!'

'How cheap?'

'Ninety pounds to you.'

'Does it work?'

'Perfect working order. I bought it off an old lady. Been going for years, on the wall of her cottage. I've had it going for two weeks on the wall of my caravan. Keeps perfect time. My watch stopped and I didn't bother to wind it up, this clock keeps such good time . . .'

Everyone was watching Lucy. She hesitated; she didn't want to hurt the man's feelings, even if his eyes were as expressionless as a great white shark's. Finally she took a picture down off a nail in the wall. 'Let's see how it looks there,' she said; and took the clock from his reluctant hands and hung it on the nail. 'Now, if you'll give me the pendulum . . .'

At that point the glass came out of the face of the clock. It didn't fall and break. It sort of wafted down, like a piece of transparent paper, and flopped on the floor.

'I had to replace the glass,' said the Great White Shark. 'It was broken, like. This is near-glass. Far better – doesn't break like glass.' He picked it up and stuffed it inside the brass bezel again. 'There y'are – good as new.'

'Pendulum, please!' Lucy kept her face very straight.

Reluctantly he gave it to her. 'No need to test it. It goes like a bomb.'

Lucy hung the pendulum, and gave it a tap to get it swinging. Immediately the hands of the clock began to go round.

Backwards. At enormous speed. About an hour a second. The works within revved like a young motorbike; the strike clanged non-stop, like a burglar alarm.

102

'Does go like a bomb,' said Trev. 'What time does it explode?'

But the Great White Shark just shook his head, as if deeply baffled. 'It was going fine in my caravan this morning.'

At which point the sheet of near-glass fell out again.

'I think I have enough clocks in my shop at the moment,' said Lucy politely. 'But thanks very much for fetching it.'

'You can have it for sixty-five,' said the man. 'It's a good goer; honest!'

'Come and join us,' said Lucy to change the subject. 'Have a drink. Only . . . could you please take your clock away? I can't hear myself think!'

'Fifty. Fifty to you,' said the Shark. 'Special offer. I like everybody to be happy . . .'

June came over and gave him a drink.

'Forty,' said the Shark, very unhappily. 'Thirty-five?'

To her amazement, Lucy saw Trev give a nod, over the heads of the crowd.

'Done,' she said, and gave the man his money.

'I'm the man to come to, for clocks,' he said. 'I get all sorts of good clocks.' And he plunged away into the crowd without a twitch of embarrassment, as the near-glass fell out of the clock for the third time.

People closed round Lucy, smiling at her, touching her arm. It was as if she'd passed some great test.

'His name's Danny Lucas,' muttered June. 'He's all right really. If you know how to handle him.'

'He has a good eye,' muttered Lesley. 'He does bring in the strangest things, but he has a dealer's eye.'

'I'm just not quite sure which is his *dealer's* eye,' said Vera cattily. 'Both his eyes give me the willies. I always think he's going to cut my throat.'

'Only financially, dear, only financially,' said Lesley. 'I *think*.'

'I can mend that clock for you,' whispered Trev. 'I think I know what's the matter with it. He's left out one of the wheels in the going-train. And new glass will only cost you a fiver. Or I'll buy it off you if you like. For forty. That's five quid quick profit. It's a good clock really.'

Lucy could've hugged him, his smile was so warm. She felt she could've hugged them all. She suddenly felt part of a great new family, warm and safe. Accepted. She loved all their faces; their jokes were the best in the world.

'Open another bottle,' she said euphorically. 'Let's all get drunk.'

It was at that moment that June said, 'I've got something for you. A parcel. The postman left it with me this morning, while you were out. I'll just nip next door an' get it.'

Everyone watched her go; everyone watched her return.

'It's got OHMS on it,' said June. 'I hope it's not the bloody Income Tax. Or the VAT?'

Everyone shuddered, and looked at the fat brown parcel in June's hand. But no one shuddered as much as Lucy. The printing on the parcel was Daddy's.

She made herself say, very casually, 'Oh, it's the Imperial War Museum. I sent for some brochures.'

Because everyone was looking at her, she made herself throw it down carelessly on a small gateleg table by the door, and drifted away to replenish people's drinks.

But for all the rest of the party, she could not keep her eyes off it. It hypnotized her as if it were a snake, and she a poor rabbit. It ruined everything. Suddenly her lovely new warm family became a scarcely bearable bunch of half-drunk people being excessively silly. Why *should* she laugh at their in-jokes? None of them were funny in the least. Did they intend to stay all night? Even the polite smiling faces of the Patels, come to view their clock once again, didn't warm her heart.

104

They all straggled away at last, long after the shops normally closed, vowing eternal friendship and haggling over things they wanted to buy from each other. Even to those who had actually bought things from her shop, Lucy could only be coolly and unconvincingly friendly.

Even then, June and Trev lingered, to discuss what a good party it had been, and who had said what, and who had got drunkest.

'You're *in*!' said June to her, enthusiastically. 'Everyone liked you, *and* your stuff.'

'I'm *whacked*,' said Lucy meaningfully.

'Me and Trev'll wash up an' pack the glasses . . .'

'No, leave them,' said Lucy, unable to keep sharpness out of her voice. 'I'll do them later. I want to put my feet up now. What a *noise* they all made!'

June looked at her sharply. 'You all right?'

'Just *tired*.' Would June never take the hint?

'You do look tired,' said June. 'OK, we'll shove off.'

They went, a little silent suddenly, a little hurt. Lucy felt mean, for having spoilt their small happiness.

Then the shop door closed behind them. But she mustn't dash for the parcel. They were still looking back at her over their shoulders, through the shop window, a little worried for her.

She waved and smiled to reassure them. One after the other, they drove away, waving back.

Only then did she dive for the parcel. It had disappeared altogether several times during the party. People had sat on it, spilt drinks on it. Somebody had even made a rough sketch of a Welsh dresser on it, and written '£1100' and 'Pawley and Hutchins, 5 Bolton Road, Blackburn'.

But now it was in her hands, making her fingers tingle like an electric shock. Now it was all hers.

She looked suspiciously up and down the road, to make

sure nobody was watching. But Barnston Road held only the usual parked cars and a black and white dog, carefully checking, then peeing against, their wheels.

She locked her door, turned the sign to say 'Closed' and dashed upstairs.

She stared at the parcel. It was addressed 'R. King, 7 Barnston Rd., Thraleby, W. Yorks'. Just enough address to get it to her; Daddy was giving nothing away. And it carried the additional official stamp of Daddy's public relations department, which sent out an endless flood of bumf to all and sundry, MPs, journalists, academic researchers. Daddy had hidden his needle in the haystack very cleverly. It warmed her heart. Daddy would outwit them yet . . .

But was she to open it? Did he mean her to open it? He hadn't said so. But there might be a letter for her inside.

With instructions . . .

But once she opened it, that would make her guilty of conspiracy in a court of law. And Daddy didn't want that. And, with a tremor in her heart, she didn't want it either . . .

She writhed in indecision for a long time.

But in the end, she had to know. Not to know was unbearable.

She spent a long time in the kitchen, with a steaming kettle and a sharp narrow knife with a point that would not stop trembling.

There was no letter from Daddy. Just sheafs and sheafs of A4 photocopying, rather cockeyed as if done by inexperienced and nervous fingers. The smell of new photocopying came faintly to her nostrils, like the smell of Daddy's fear.

And there was one more thing, which fell out of the parcel as she shook it despairingly. Half a sheet of paper, torn roughly across. Scribbled, in pencil, Daddy's most careless handwriting. A list, every item of which ended in a question mark.

> New York Times?
> Washington Post?
> Figaro?
> Paris Match?
> France Soir?
> Allgemeine Zeitung?
> Il Tempo?
> National Examiner?
> Greenpeace?

The people Daddy was going to blow the whistle to.

But what did the scribbled sheet mean? Was this merely Daddy thinking on paper? A memo to himself, like he so often made? Or was it some kind of instruction to her? What was she supposed to *do* about it?

Baffled, she turned back to the mass of photocopying. Departmental memos, full of abbreviations, only a few of which she understood. DTI, DOE, EEC . . . but the rest she'd never heard of. She gave up pretty quickly. And sheaves and sheaves of statistics. And she had a horror of statistics; especially statistics about abbreviations. Graphs, briefings, they simply swam before her uncomprehending eyes. Only one of the last sheets made any kind of sense. Second draft of the Beardsley-Houghton Report on International Whale Stocks. Again, she could not take the statistics; the figures blurred together meaninglessly. But she read the summary, the last paragraph. Whale-stocks seemed to have recovered beyond expectation. The International Moratorium on Whaling was working. The great whales were going to survive and flourish after all.

She was glad about that. She'd always been miserable

about whaling. What had that red-spattered poster in the back of Mr Trent's car at school said?

STOP THE BLOODY WHALING.

Well, it had stopped, and that was good. And stopping it had worked, and that was better still.

But it was hardly vital state secrets, was it? She wondered again, with a sneaking unease, whether poor Daddy was really going potty . . .

But the human mind can only take so much. She was very tired, and she still had the shop to clear up, after the party. Let Daddy get on with it, whatever it was. It wasn't really her concern. She put all the stuff back into the parcel carefully, and fetched a tube of glue and carefully stuck back the flap of the envelope. One end would *not* stick down properly. She squeezed too much glue under it, and when she hammered it flat with her fist, a little of the glue spurted out again.

It left a tiny dark mark she could not get rid of; which spoilt the innocence of the sealed envelope, and threw her into a tizzy of rage and panic.

Steady on, girl. You're tired, that's all. Leave it. Who's to know who made the glue mark? She took the parcel back upstairs to her bedroom and put it on her dressing-table. She ought to wash up . . . she ought to cook a meal . . .

In the end she just curled up on the bed and fell asleep.

Chapter Twelve

The next morning, she felt better. The parcel had shrunk to being just a parcel. Sunlight was streaming into the shop, and it was good to be among her polished things.

She was having an inward private smile at a middle-aged couple in the shop. The woman wore a light fur coat, and the man a camel-hair overcoat. They were obviously well-off; and knew about antiques, from the reverent way they handled everything. He seemed more interested in brass, and she in china. Several times Lucy thought each was going to buy something. But at the moment of decision, with the object in their hands possessively, the other partner would say, 'Oh, come on, we're late. Maisie's expecting us. We're half an hour late already . . .'

Then the object would be put down, unbought. But they wouldn't leave the shop. Instead, they would wander on to something else.

They were never going to buy anything. But, as they circled and circled, they pleased Lucy; like the little carved man and woman on a Black Forest barometer who emerged from their house alternately, signifying sun or rain. She had never known a couple so pleasingly odd.

Then she heard the whistling of the approaching postman and, looking through the window, she saw he was carrying a long brown packet.

She just knew it was from Daddy. She froze.

The postman came in. She knew him well by this time. He was called Stan, and he was little and stocky with ginger hair. Always whistling, and had a grin for you, rain or shine. He could turn even a bill from British Telecom into a festival; he could turn no post at all into a festival with an apologetic 'Nothing for you today, m'dear' and a fatherly twinkle and a joke or a bit of kindly gossip about some old lady further down the street.

He was twinkling at her now. 'OHMS again? Two in two days? You a personal mate of the Prime Minister? Or Prince Edward's girl-friend?'

She forced a smile for him. 'Oh, it's just stuff from the Imperial War Museum.'

He frowned; turned over the parcel, puzzled. 'Funny! The Imperial War Museum's stuff usually has their own address on it!'

She blushed, at being caught in her lie. Everyone in the shop was watching her now, expecting an explanation. She felt like a condemned criminal. Afterwards, they would remember; afterwards, they might give evidence . . . *Damn* Daddy!

'Oh, I don't know,' she snapped. 'They must know their own business best.'

Stan quailed at the look on her face. The brightness faded out of him. He looked baffled, hurt. Then went without a word. Again, he would remember.

The couple kept on giving her curious looks; then left the shop abruptly. Oh, damn, damn, damn!

She locked the door, turned the sign to 'Closed' and retired to the kitchen, to steam the packet open.

Still no letter from Daddy. Just more photocopying. DTI this time. Schedules of factories to be built; in Durham, South Wales, Birmingham. Cars, tellies, computers . . .

Well, that was good news; the kind of good news the Prime Minister would be happy to announce in Parliament. Lots of new jobs for the unemployed. What the hell

110

was Daddy up to, stealing good news and calling it wicked?

Again, she wondered uneasily if he was going potty, as she re-glued the envelope and put it with the other, and tried to forget it. Opened the shop again, and waited for people to distract her.

But it clouded over and began to rain. June said rain was bad for trade. People stayed indoors, instead of going for a walk and looking in shop windows.

June had gone to a sale at a dead man's house. She had wrinkled up her nose and said it wasn't the kind of sale Lucy would enjoy. In her absence, the shop seemed a dull grey prison. Full of one question. Was Daddy going mad?

The shop bell clanged, making her jump. It was a fat spotty shaggy-haired youth, in a soaking green anorak that dripped water everywhere. He examined everything in the shop with a dull disgusted look, then asked if she sold secondhand fishing-tackle. She just shook her head mutely, and he banged the door behind him bad-temperedly. And she went back to wondering if Daddy was going potty.

Shop bell again. The woman who ran the village cake shop. Another regular who was never going to buy anything. She only came to chatter. At least she wasn't nosy. Too full of her own problems. All you had to do was listen and nod; though her voice drilled right through your skull.

'I always liked cooking I liked cooking for my kids when they lived at home but when they left I didn't have the same incentive you see I mean there's not much point to doing fancy cooking for two so I thought I'd try opening a cake shop I mean it would get me out of the house and among people because it's very quiet on your own at home when your kids have gone and at least the shop's a bit of life and bit of pin-money goodness knows you need every penny you can raise these days with the prices . . .'

It had seemed quite interesting, the first time Lucy had

heard it . . . Lucy wondered what the woman would do if she, Lucy, suddenly began screaming her head off. But she just gritted her teeth and in the end the woman left.

The last customers were worst. Kevin and his mum. Kevin was three, and said to be the image of his dad. Lucy could well believe it. With his blond hair and sulky good looks and total disobedience, Kevin was the youngest male chauvinist pig Lucy had ever met. He touched everything in the shop, in spite of endlessly being told not to. He handled things with the same disregard he showed to his new model fire-engine, which he used as a roller-skate, grinding its wheels, which had already lost their tyres, round and round Lucy's polished tile floor, with a series of horrible gratings and screechings.

Kevin's mum (whose name Lucy had never learnt) was about twenty, pregnant again, and droopy with it. She gave vent to sheeplike bleats.

'Keviiin! Put that down, our Kevin!'

'Put that down, Kevin, or I'll *smack* you!'

But Kevin ground on inexorably, unsmacked and undaunted. Lucy comforted herself by remembering that he hadn't actually broken anything on his three previous invasions. He seemed more keen on breaking *her* nerve, with a subtly orchestrated series of clinks and thuds. Then he stood up on the rocking-chair in the window, and rocked alarmingly; the chair tapping gently, at the end of every rock, against a tripod table full of expensive ruby glass that jumped slightly in sympathy, a kind of chorus of tinks . . .

His mother wondered if Kevin would become an acrobat when he grew up; he was so well co-ordinated and could judge things so well. Lucy silently hoped he'd become a high-wire trapeze artist and break his little neck.

'Pity you're not married,' said Kevin's mum. 'Children keep you young and lively . . . I don't know what I did with my life, until Kevin came . . .'

112

At quarter to five, Lucy said she was locking up early because of the rain, and edged Kevin's mum out on to the pavement on the fourth attempt.

She felt utterly drained. Everything was falling apart. This shop was never going to work; nobody was going to buy anything from her ever again. And Daddy wasn't any kind of noble hero; just a hopeless nut on his way to the funny farm. And her own attempts at finding a hidey-hole were pathetic, when even an ordinary little postman could see through her lies . . .

She locked the door and fled upstairs, before June could return full of the little treasures she'd found at the sale. She just couldn't face June and her little treasures tonight. She put her bedside lamp on the floor, where June wouldn't notice its glow, even in the stormy dusk; and lay on the bed, fists clenched, legs screwed up, worrying about Daddy. The rain beat endlessly on the windowpanes; the room felt more and more cold and damp, yet she couldn't summon up the energy to switch on Big Artie's old fan-heater. Was that a new damp patch on the ceiling, breaking through her lovely new paint? Her whole ridiculous new life was crumbling . . .

She must distract herself. There was an old browning tabloid newspaper still lining the drawer of her bedside cabinet . . . Dispiritedly she skimmed the pages. Drug problems of pop-stars. Love-lives of *Coronation Street*. Disgusted with herself, she flipped another page.

A gentle elderly face peered out at her. A thin old lady in a headscarf, bending over a plant, yet smiling at the camera. The caption read 'Mrs Hilda Murrell among the roses she loved.'

The headline above screamed:

WHO KILLED HILDA MURRELL?

113

She read on, appalled. Hilda Murrell, octogenarian Shrewsbury rose-grower and nature-lover, had been attacked while alone in her country house. Pursued and dragged from room to room, battered senseless. Then loaded into her own car, and dumped in a field to die of exposure.

No robbery. No sexual assault. No motive. Police baffled.

But the writer of the article wasn't at all baffled. He'd dug up a lot of new facts.

Hilda Murrell's nephew was an ex-naval officer, who knew far too much about the sinking of the Argentine cruiser *General Belgrano* in the Falklands War . . .

Hilda Murrell herself was busy preparing a devastating paper to read at the inquiry into the building of the Sizewell B atomic reactor . . .

Hilda Murrell, the writer said, was a thorn in the flesh of the Government. Who had been got rid of.

By MI5, posing as a psychopathic killer.

Oh, this is just the gutter-press talking, thought Lucy. You can't trust a word they say. Gutter-sensationalism, Daddy called it. She despised the gutter-press utterly.

But she read on.

MI5, the writer said, could get away with anything. Illegal bugging of Labour Government phones had been proved, back in the seventies. Burglary. Murder of opponents. They were ruthless criminals, protected by a criminal government. With the police warned to look the other way . . .

Come, said Lucy to herself, dismiss this rubbish from your mind. But then she heard Daddy's voice saying, almost as if he was in the bedroom with her, 'Our Lords and Masters have been very wicked, and I'm going to blow the whistle on them.'

If Daddy called the Government wicked, they must be . . . if Daddy was not going mad. And she didn't think he was going mad . . .

Oh, she did not know what to think.

This newspaper was old, old. What had the death of some unknown old lady to do with her? It happened yonks ago.

And yet the old lady's face kept drifting before her closed eyes.

She was dead. *Someone* had killed her. That much must be true.

And the police had never caught the culprit . . .

Daddy was becoming a thorn in the flesh of the Government . . .

She went over and over it, and each time her mind went a little bit faster, until her own brain was spinning like a wheel, and she did not know what she believed.

It was a long time before her body had mercy on her and she slept.

When she awakened, it was pitch dark, and for an awful moment she didn't know where she was. Then she recognized the dark blue shape of the window, with the crack in one corner. Her watch said 9.15. Her body felt like lead, but she made herself get up and put on the overhead light and draw the curtains. The sixty-watt bulb seemed to fill the room with darkness.

She was alone. With the phone.

The phone that might ring at any moment, and explode her world into a thousand fragments. Not a phone, but a bomb. It leered at her with its single round white eye.

Alone.

With the phone.

She could go for a walk or a drive. But it would still be there when she got back.

Besides, she dare not leave it.

She and the phone would be alone, all night. She knew she would not sleep again. She knew she could not bear it.

She wanted a human voice. A voice that would understand.

Daddy.

Aunt Maude.

Claire.

The Samaritans.

No, no, no, no, no, no.

Mr Betts.

She had talked to him once, after Mummy died. In the privacy of his little room. She had said the unsayable to him. That she didn't believe in God; that she hated God. She had wept. He had listened and nodded and kept her secrets.

She knew she must not ring him. But his image grew huge in her mind, and in it there was a little comfort, the only comfort in the whole world. And, with a glint of self-indulgence, she thought she would ring Directory Enquiries and get his number.

When they answered, she could hardly get his name out, let alone remember his address. Her mouth would hardly move, as if she had lockjaw.

'Mr C. F. S. Betts, 25 Romney Terrace,' said the operator, full of patient triumph, as if she'd cracked the riddle of the Rosetta Stone. '081 834 29854.' Then Lucy found she had nothing to write with, and stumbled downstairs screaming the number out loud at the top of her voice, lest she forget it.

Now she had his number, the power of Mr Betts grew monstrous. The phone drew her hand like a magnet, no matter how often she pulled it back.

She didn't have to *speak* to him; it would be enough to just hear his voice. It *couldn't* do any harm if she didn't speak; if she kept her hand tight over the mouthpiece. It would be enough to know he was still in the world . . .

She dialled the number with bated breath, earpiece pressed so hard against her ear it really hurt.

'29854,' came his voice down the phone, so warm and gruff and like him she could almost smell his tobacco-smoke breath. She clenched the mouthpiece harder, trying to control her breathing.

He said '29854,' again. Then, 'Chris Betts speaking.' A little baffled. She was sad to be annoying him; he sounded a bit tired. But every syllable was like food and drink.

Then he said, with a spurt of irritation, 'Oh, stop messing about! Is that someone from school?'

Jolted into obedience, she said, 'Yes,' in a very small voice.

'Lucy?' he said. 'Is that Lucy?'

How could he know, from one 'yes'? It made him seem a magician. It made her feel so much loved that tears started into her eyes, and she said 'yes' again because it was like coming home.

'What's the matter, Lucy?'

What could she say?

'Are you still worried about that exam? I *told* you you were going to be all right.' He sighed in exasperation. 'Oh, you girls . . .'

Why couldn't she lie to him, say 'yes'? But she *couldn't* lie to him. And anyway, he would *know*. And the tears were streaming down her face, and her throat kept swallowing. All because his voice made her feel so safe; so safe that all the pain came flooding out.

'It's *not* the exam, is it?' he asked, curiously definite. 'Is it . . . your mother? Would you like to come round and talk about it?' He sounded just a little weary again.

117

All she could do was sniff and gulp.

'Lucy . . . you're not . . . in real trouble . . . are you?' His voice grew wary. He must be wondering if she'd got herself pregnant. 'Shall I come round to you? My car's still in the drive . . .'

That got her throat functioning again.

'NO!' The thought of him going round to the house made her mind work like lightning. 'No, I'm not at home. I'm up north . . .'

'On holiday? Lucy . . . you're not *homesick*?' There was a tinge of disappointment now. But it got her off the hook. All she had to do was sniff and say nothing and let him think he was right.

'You're on your own? Not with your father? I saw him in the hypermarket a couple of days ago. Not to speak to. I thought he looked tired . . .' Good old Bettsy, worrying about everyone in the world.

'Mmm,' she said. She *was* on her own.

'You with people you know? Are they nice?'

'Mmm,' she said again, thinking of June and Trev and Big Artie.

'What's the bother, then? Haven't you been away from home before? On you own? I mean, you'd better get this sorted out before Cambridge. You'll have to make new friends there . . .'

And now it was all right, because he was launched on a flood of friendly advice about homesickness, all totally irrelevant. But his voice was like a warm shower, his concern for her like a wide warm sea, and she luxuriated in it. By the end, a couple of things he said had her laughing in spite of herself.

After the second laugh, he yawned and said, 'You sound a bit better.'

'I am. Thanks.'

'You don't want me to have a word with your father . . .'

'NO!' Her treacherous voice shot up an octave. Then she added lamely, 'This holiday has cost him a lot of money. And I don't want to worry him.'

Both of which were true.

He yawned again, a homely comforting sound. 'The first time away from home's the worst. You'll get used to it. Then you'll be set up for Cambridge. Better to be homesick now than homesick there . . . Where are you staying, by the way?'

He had given her the strength to lie to him.

'Scarborough.'

'Nice part of the country. But watch out for Dracula!'

And then he was gone. She listened to the resumed dialling code a long time, as if she could hear the echo of his voice in it. Then she put down the receiver.

And slept.

Chapter Thirteen

She wakened early, about half-past six. She felt dirty and revolting, from sleeping in her clothes. But her mind was clear. She pulled back big Artie's thin curtains and let the rising sun hit her full in the face. The bright light was like food for her soul.

The street outside was quiet, empty most of the time. That soothed her too, made her feel ahead of the day. There were sparrows pecking their breakfast of grass-seeds from a solitary pile of horse-droppings left yesterday by a solitary girl rider from the riding school further up the poor little valley. The sparrows flew away every time a car passed, but came back determinedly.

Somehow it made her want to have another go at the contents of Daddy's packets. Maybe this time she could make some sense of them. Maybe something would settle once and for all the fear that Daddy was potty.

Two men passed, going to work on their bikes. One was smoking a pipe. Bettsy smoked a pipe on his bike. This morning she felt still full of Bettsy's voice. It kept her hands steady as she re-opened the envelopes.

For a long time, she got nowhere. The photocopies were so technical and boring her mind kept bouncing off them, wanting to turn on the radio, or have breakfast, or just be happy instead.

But, at the bottom of the second packet, she came across the survey about whales again.

Surely that was in the first packet? Had she muddled them up? No, there was a copy of it in each packet. She laid them side by side, and checked they were the same.

With a sharply indrawn breath, she saw they weren't. They looked the same, but nearly every figure had been altered.

The first copy noted less than four thousand right whales in the North Atlantic.

The second noted over ten thousand.

Her eyes flew from figure to figure, comparing. Nearly every figure in the second copy was much much higher.

She checked the dates on the two surveys. They were the same.

Somebody was fiddling the figures.

In that instant, she knew Daddy was not going mad. A great gladness gripped her by the throat, as she stood by the window again, drinking in the rising sun.

Then she felt so guilty for ever having doubted him. Poor Daddy, didn't he have enough troubles without a disloyal daughter? She must help him now, in any way she could. Make up for it. But how?

Once he was on the run, he would have to hide. Not show his face in public. How could he get his documents photo-copied? How could he buy envelopes . . . take them to the post office? All this she could do for him. All this she would do for him. Today. Sooner the better.

Now she had something definite to do, she felt full of energy.

Handling June was easy; June owed her a favour from yesterday and June was always one for repaying a favour.

'I'm going out buying,' she said to June. 'Will you watch my shop for me?' As she had been meant to watch June's shop yesterday; open it up if anyone wanted to buy anything. Not that anybody had.

June looked a bit anxious. 'Want me to come with you?'

'I'm a big girl now. Time I tackled your northern thugs on my own . . .'

'Always beat Harry Brimble down twenty-five per cent; he expects it. And watch Flora . . .'

Lucy groaned inwardly. June would ask them all about her visit. So she said briskly, 'I was thinking of trying further afield. I know everything *they've* got – I'm a bit sick of it. I feel like a change . . .'

'Aye,' said June thoughtfully, eyeing the ridge of hills across the valley. 'I know how you feel. You get restless, cooped up all day.'

Lucy felt rotten. June must think her a spoilt young madam . . .

'I thought I'd try Skipton and Ilkley.'

June began to reel off a list of dealers round Skipton and Ilkley.

Lucy fled.

It looked just what Lucy wanted: a little Victorian public library in a leafy suburb, twenty miles away from June. Only two cars parked outside.

She'd worked out that libraries were better for photo-copying than shops. Shopkeepers took the photocopying off you and went into a back room where they probably had a good nosy. Libraries just turned your note into 10p coins and left you to get on with it.

She was dressed as a student. Hair up and spectacles, but jeans and sweater and her school scarf, which was gaudy enough to pass for a college scarf. She got out the boring

Japanese factory stuff to start with. People, all sorts of people, got worked up over whales.

The library was totally empty; the two females librarians watched her all the way from the door with avid interest. They were bored, had nothing else to think about but her. Alarm-bells began to ring inside Lucy's head, but it was too late. She was committed.

'Good morning.' She creaked her mouth into a smile.

One of the women was a harmless old wrinkly, the sort she'd been expecting in a place like this. The other was formidable, not much over forty. Expensive ethnic blouse, streaked grey hair, large fashionable metal-rim spectacles and a determined unsmiling mouth. The sort of woman who might have a son or daughter at university; who might have been to university herself.

'Can I use your photocopier, please?'

The woman looked more disapproving than ever. 'People fool about with it, break it. I can do some photocopies *for* you. What do you want photocopied?' She almost snatched the stuff from Lucy's hand. 'This isn't stuff from this library, is it? We're only supposed to photocopy stuff from this library . . .'

'Oh, well . . .' Lucy reached for her papers back, with a feeling of relief.

'However,' said the woman, 'I'll make an exception in your case.' She was busy reading the top page. 'This is government stuff; isn't there a copyright in force?'

'It's only for my thesis,' said Lucy desperately. 'They let you.'

'Oh, you're a *student*, are you? Which university?'

'Sunderland Poly.' The woman looked much too grand to have anybody at Sunderland Poly.

The woman's lip curled in reassuring disgust. 'Whatever

123

did you go *there* for? Well, I suppose beggars can't be choosers. What are you reading?'

'Business studies.'

Again the woman's lip curled. But she led the way down the empty sunlit aisles calling behind her, 'You can manage the desk on your own, Mrs Collyhurst?'

'Yes,' replied Mrs Collyhurst in a humble crushed voice.

A cloud of dust-motes flew into the air, as the cover came off the photocopier. Lucy only hoped it still worked, after such disuse.

'One copy of each?'

'Nine,' said Lucy.

'Nine?' The woman looked at her hard, with those pale grey pin-point eyes. 'What on earth do you want *nine* copies for?'

'There are others in my group,' faltered Lucy. 'And we have to cut them up. It spoils them.' Then she added, she didn't quite know why, 'My boyfriend wants three copies.'

'So your *boyfriend* lets you do all the work. Typical.'

But a strange change had come over the woman's face, as she said the word 'boyfriend'. A softening of the harsh lines, a dilation of the pupils of the eyes, so they seemed a darker grey. The tiny tip of the woman's tongue came out and wet her lips. Her fierceness was replaced by a look of cloying nosiness. At the same time, her well-manicured hand with its short nails fed the first sheet in, and pressed a button, and the machine spewed out nine clean copies. Then, as she was feeding in the second sheet, she said, 'I suppose your boyfriend lets you do all the *cooking* for him too?'

But the look in her eyes said 'sex'.

Nine more copies spewed out. But then the woman appeared to be reading the third sheet. 'I didn't know the Japs were building car factories in Birmingham. My husband's in the motor trade. I'm sure he would have told me.' Her eyes were needle-sharp again.

Lucy played her trump card. 'I don't do *all* the cooking for my boyfriend. Only when I stay the night . . .'

The effect of that statement on the woman's eyes was quite remarkable. She began to blink rapidly. But her thumb pressed the button, as if of its own volition, and nine more copies spewed out. Her hand appeared to have acquired a life of its own, doing the photocopying at an enormous rate, while her eyes seemed to devour Lucy. 'Stay the *night*?'

'You know,' said Lucy, 'after an all-night party. We all bring sleeping bags and sleep on the lounge floor.'

'Oh,' said the woman. She sounded *very* disappointed. Her attention began to drift back towards the papers.

'My boyfriend's very *demanding*,' said Lucy. 'Sex is a terrible problem . . .'

'How do you mean?' asked the woman, avidly, as nine more lovely sheets spewed out. Lucy noticed there were only three pages to go.

'Well . . . AIDS,' she said. 'It does put you off the idea.'

'Oh, yes, AIDS,' said the woman, her voice again dull with disappointment. The photocopying hand faltered; again her eyes began to drift towards the documents.

'My boyfriend was only saying in bed last night . . .'

The photocopying hand brisked up again, while the woman's dark grey eyes hung on Lucy's face expectantly horrified.

'Were you in *bed* with him?'

One more sheet to go.

'Oh, no,' said Lucy. 'He's staying at our house. In the vac. He got a heavy cold, so my mother sent him to bed. I was bringing him a hot whisky and lemon . . .'

'Oh.' But the last sheet was triumphantly through. The

woman stacked them all together neatly, but hung on to them as if they were the Crown Jewels.

'Could we hurry up, please,' said Lucy. 'I have a dentist's appointment at eleven.'

That got them back to the desk. But the woman was still far too interested in the documents, trying to read them while pretending to count them.

'Of course my boyfriend's got some very peculiar habits,' said Lucy. 'It's because he's a foreigner . . .'

'A foreigner?' The woman's lips fell open. 'What *sort* of foreigner?' She let Lucy twitch the sheets from her nerveless fingers.

'Oh, only German,' said Lucy, exalting. 'But he eats smelly things like bierwurst and sauerkraut. They make his breath *stink*! That's nine copies each, of nineteen sheets. How much is that?'

Defeated, the woman moved to her desk-top calculator.

She had the business pretty well sussed out, by the time she came to the whales, at the end. She chose a big busy city library, after four o'clock, when the housewives were finishing off their shopping by changing their books, and the schoolkids were piling in, full of eager enquiries, and running the staff off their feet. By this time, she was Pat Furlong, student marine biologist at Liverpool University. She demanded books about whales; lots of reference books about whales. She scoured the microfiche system for them; sweating, grumbling and dusty assistants bore huge tomes to her table in the reference library. She went on and on to people about the plight of whales till their eyes glazed over. When they were sick of the sight of her, she requested the use of the photocopier. They left her well alone.

The trouble now was that everyone else seemed to want

126

to use the photocopier, to copy posters for car-boot sales, records of their ancestor's death from cholera in 1867, numbers of cow-hides tanned in that city in 1902. She had to keep breaking off and giving way to people who humbly wanted 'just one of this' and then seemed suddenly to need a hundred. And the machine kept breaking down, and a little man kept being summoned from some back room, to talk to the machine and slap it with fierce familiarity, as if it was his wayward child.

Still, the library had a marvellous reference book, with the address of every newspaper in the world in it, so she spent her waiting-times patiently copying out the addresses of the newspapers Daddy wanted.

She was just finishing when she felt somebody staring at her. In the end, she *had* to look up to see who it was.

It was a total stranger, a tall thin youth whose long fair hair badly needed washing, but who stared at her with huge innocent gentle blue eyes.

'I see you're interested in whales,' he said, with a slight and touching stammer. 'I'd like to talk to you about whales. You know the Japs and the Icelanders are still killing them; and the terrible things they do to dolphins in the Faeroes . . . ? Can I buy you a coffee when you've finished?'

Without blinking an eyelid, she said, 'Got half an hour's work to do yet. See you in the entrance in half an hour?'

'Thanks,' he said, and gave her the loveliest smile. 'I'll look forward to it.' And sloped away with a beatific look on his face.

He was standing waiting for her, as she drove past in the car. Patiently, hopefully, as if he would wait for ever. He looked so nice and trusting, and she would never even know his name . . .

'Bitch,' she said to herself as she accelerated round the corner, and out of his life for ever. 'Cow! Lying slut!'

But really she felt high, triumphant. Lucy, late doormat, now master-spy. On the way home, she bought nine big jiffy-bags. The one thing she forgot was to call at any antique-shops. She didn't even remember till June came running out eagerly from her shop, to see what she'd got.

Lucy shook her head and pulled a face. 'Pricey, all of it. And a right load of old tat.'

'I could have told you,' said June sympathetically. 'Skipton and Ilkley are tourist-traps. You never get a bargain in a pretty town. I nearly told you, but I thought you'd better find out for yourself. Best try Rochdale next time. Fancy a cup of tea?' And she launched straight into what Flora had done to Big Artie now, and what Jessie had said about it.

She had spent all evening sorting out the photocopying; checking it over and over again. It would not do to make the slightest mistake where the *New York Times* and, even more, *Il Tempo* was concerned.

Now each set of photocopying lay in its addressed jiffy-bag. She had pondered long whether to address it to 'The Political Editor' or 'The Economic Editor' and in the end decided to put both for safety. Daddy could change it if he wanted to . . .

The jiffy-bags gleamed dully along the bed in a neat row. They looked a bit like a row of missiles, under an aeroplane's wing. Missiles to bring down a government. But had mere *paper* any power? Or would they be tossed in the wastebin, unread?

But she was sure Daddy would add covering letters, explaining everything. Fuses to prime the missiles . . .

Daddy, Daddy, where are you? She looked at the phone, but it just crouched in the corner, mute.

Then it suddenly rang, as if it was a living thing that could read her thoughts.

But it was only June.

'Can you open up the shop for me in the morning, love? Our Dennis's slipped his disc again, and I've got to run him to the doctor's. I'll be in by eleven, I expect. Our Tim'll drop the key through your letter-box, on his way to the pub tonight . . .'

Lucy stored away her missiles in a neat pile on her dressing-table, and went to boil a kettle to wash away the old sweat of the day.

Chapter Fourteen

The cardboard box lay on Lucy's desk, between her and the old lady. In despair, Lucy stared at the contents. Dusty non-matching cups and saucers, nearly all chipped. A cracked jug with roses on it; an aluminium contraption for slicing hard-boiled eggs. In a word, rubbish. A couple of the prettier unchipped saucers might sell at fifty pence, for ash-trays . . .

'I only need five pounds for them,' quavered the old lady. 'They were our Emily's things. I'm clearing out her cottage. She died last week. She was the only sister I had left, and once there were six of us.' She picked up the cracked jug and stroked it lovingly. 'This was her favourite. Many a time I've seen her pour milk from this, when we had a cup of tea . . .'

'Perhaps you ought to keep it, to remember her by?' suggested Lucy, hopelessly.

'Haven't got the room, love. Got all my other sisters' things in the cupboard. And it's hard to manage on a pension. I had to pay for Emily's funeral myself. She couldn't afford the insurance.'

Lucy made herself look the old lady in the face, steeling herself to say 'no'. But that old withered face suddenly crinkled up, and a solitary tear trickled down towards the stray whiskers on her upper lip.

It was impossible to say no. How could you tell an old lady that her dead sister's stuff was worthless rubbish? Who could be so heartless? The cuffs of the old lady's coat were frayed; her hands had the knobbles of arthritis.

Lucy reached for her purse and gave her a five-pound note.

'Bless you, love! Good luck wi' your new business. God bless you!' And the old lady was gone.

Lucy stood there, wearily picking through the things. One of the saucers she'd hoped to sell was faintly but irredeemably cracked, when she rubbed the grime off it with her thumb.

Oh, well, she'd comforted a very sad and lonely old lady. It's just like giving to Oxfam, really. But what could she do with this rubbish? She hadn't the heart to tip it in the dustbin. It would be like tipping dead Emily into the dustbin . . .

She was still painfully hovering when June came in, bearing two mugs of coffee, the usual fag stuck in one corner of her mouth.

'Our Dennis'll live, the doctor reckons. Muscular stress of the mid-back. He's been out up the fields wi' that Doreen Harborne, *I* reckon. He wasn't home till one in the morning . . .'

Then she took one look at the cardboard box and said, 'Oh God – Mourning Meg. I meant to warn you about her, but I forgot. I thought I saw her drive off, when I was parking. She's gotta new Astra.'

'Mourning Meg? New Astra?' yelped Lucy, an awful sinking feeling in her stomach.

'Don't tell me,' said June wearily. 'That load of tat is the property of her dead sister, whose cottage she is just clearing out. And when you plucked up courage to say no, she cried? How much you give her? Three quid?'

'Five,' said Lucy, blushing with shame.

'I think she scavenges the corporation tip for the stuff.

Old cow. They ought to give her an Oscar. She'd make a fortune, only she can never pull the same trick twice. She has to find new suckers all the time . . .' Nevertheless, June's fingers were busy among the rubbish, rubbing off the dirt, holding things up to the light, looking at trademarks with the avid air of a foraging squirrel. 'She sometimes turns something up – she hasn't a clue about antiques. Hey, this saucer's all right. English imitation of Chinese, about 1790. That's worth two quid, anyway.'

Lucy's heart began to heal over. She'd only lost three quid, not five.

Then her heart leapt. The phone upstairs was ringing.

'Excuse me.' Her feet thundered on the stairs.

Slowly, ruthlessly, June went on delving in the box of rubbish. She held up the aluminium egg-slicer and said, 'Quid.'

She held up a blue egg-cup shaped like a duck and said, 'Fifty pee.'

She held up a tea-spoon and said, 'LNER. Mebbe some railway buff . . .'

She rubbed the bottom of a little china sugar-bowl and said, in a voice of awe, 'Clarice Cliffe. *Real* Clarice Cliffe.'

A struggle seemed to be going on in her very soul. Finally she called upstairs, 'I'll give you back your five quid on this lot, if you like.'

Lucy called back 'Yeah' as if she couldn't care less.

June shrugged, and piled all the stuff back into the box.

'You've got a lot to learn, Rachel,' she said quietly to herself. 'I suppose it comes of having a rich daddy. I wish I had a rich daddy.' Then she shoved the box under her arm, and departed.

*

Upstairs, Lucy was talking to Daddy. A frighteningly exuberant Daddy, whom she thought had been drinking again.

'I'm in Bodmin, kitten. In Bodmin and clean away. I really diddled them. I knew they were watching the house – they were hardly bothering to hide themselves any more. So I got in Pete Holderness and all his lads. The four of them. Told him I wanted the whole house decorated outside, over the weekend. Of course Pete jumped at it, with all the overtime. He's used to obliging the rich and foolish. Anyway, they turned up first thing on Saturday morning, two vans, ladders and stuff all over the drive, painters nipping off for pasties and stuff from the yard they'd forgotten, trannies blaring, endless mugs of tea . . . I kept on nipping out with mugs of tea, so that our ever-zealous watchers wouldn't panic . . .

'I don't think they knew what had hit them. The idea of a watched suspect having his house painted . . . I'd like to see their notebooks. Anyway, I left it till Sunday afternoon, by which time they must have been sick to death of recording the comings and goings of painters, then I put on overalls myself and began painting the downstairs loo. Pete and the lads thought that a rare joke . . . called me a stinge. Then, about four o'clock, I asked Pete if I could borrow one of his vans to nip down to the shops for a video – he'd blocked my car up in the garage with all his stuff by that time, as I knew he would. He gave me the van keys, I put on a white painter's jacket and cap that I'd bought specially, picked up a painter's toolbag I'd filled with my own gear, took off my spectacles, walked out to the van whistling and just drove away. They hadn't a clue . . .

'I drove to the nearest Tube, dumped the van and the overalls, spent two hours dodging around the underground system, and here I am, gone, as the Irishman said.'

133

She felt quite overcome with his cleverness, more drunk than he was. Her head spun, but she only said, 'What are you doing in Bodmin?'

'Masquerading as a walker, kitten. Big boots, big ruck-sack, the lot. Bought a lot of stuff at Army and Navy stores, on the Monday morning. And I'm letting my beard grow. It's not bad for three days . . .'

'What are you going to do now?'

There was an uneasy silence; then he said, 'You did get my two packets?'

'Yes. Are there any more to come?'

'No. That's the lot. Just keep them safe for me. And *don't* open them, whatever you do.'

'Daddy, I . . .'

The pips went.

'Must go, kitten. No more money. Be in touch. Love you.'

Then the phone whined, and went dead.

She spent a restless night. The wind got up, and howled round the chimneys. Twice, heavy rain drummed against her window. She wondered if Daddy was out in it all. Was he keeping dry? Was he safe? She took Tibbie and the kittens to bed, and cuddled them for comfort.

She walked into June's shop next morning feeling like death warmed up. June was in her usual early morning pose, thin bottom perched on the edge of her prize piece, the mahogany wash-stand with Art Nouveau tiles. Fag in mouth, perusing *Today*.

'God,' said June, 'what's the world coming to? This big-wig's done in his own teenage daughter. My dad was only a brickie, and many a thump he gave me when I came home late. But I was never scared he might do me in. Look at her,

134

poor little thing. Nearly breaks your heart. Hardly begun to live, and now she's dead.'

She handed Lucy the paper. Lucy took it without thinking. Looked, and saw her own face. And Daddy's face. And a headline that said:

TOP CIVIL SERVANT SOUGHT: HUNT FOR MISSING GIRL

Her brain just jammed solid. She couldn't think. All kinds of explosions seemed to happen inside her. It was all she could manage to do, just stand there holding the paper. She tried to read, but it only came through in little disjointed bursts of print that did not join up together.

'The missing girl has not been seen for some weeks, since she left a friend after playing tennis . . .'

'Police are seriously concerned that the girl may no longer be alive . . .'

'William Hargreaves Smith, a Principal at the Department of Trade and Industry . . .'

'Friends said that he had never recovered from the death of his wife in a car-crash, just over a year ago. He had seemed withdrawn and moody. The possibility of a double fatality is not ruled out . . .'

'Police frogmen worked all night, dragging nearby lakes and reservoirs . . .'

She stared at her own face, which stared solemnly back. The police had used the school group-photograph taken two weeks ago. But it hadn't been a wise choice. She'd had her head down, scowling, because she hated group-photographs. It made her look pudding-faced, fatter than she really was.

'Hey, don't pinch my bloody paper,' said June. 'People are always the same. You show them one thing, and they take the paper off you and read it from cover to cover.'

Lucy gave it back to her.

135

June immediately turned it inside out and handed it back again. 'What do you think of this bargain offer?'

The bargain offer was six rose-trees which would make a hedge by growing at amazing speed. With blooms like cabbages.

A great warm tide of relief swept through Lucy. June had made no connection at all between the photograph and her own face. And if her disguise had fooled sharp-eyed June, it would fool anybody.

'Watch the shop for me, will you?' she made herself ask casually. 'I'm just nipping out for some bread and stuff.'

'Right,' said June, lost in the paper again. 'I see that stupid judge has let that rapist off. Says women who say "no" don't always mean it. I ask you. Safer to hit any amorous bloke who tries it on wi' a beer-mug. Then he'll *know* you mean it.'

Back in her bedroom, Lucy changed out of her sweater and jeans (the newspaper had mentioned sweater and jeans) and put on one of Mummy's older suits. Then she rebuilt her chignon in the most severe and disciplined way, and set off for Mr Patel's. The street was busy with shoppers. Some of whom said either 'Good morning, Miss Kingsmith,' or 'Good morning, Rachel.' Which calmed her a bit.

Mr Patel sold newspapers. The spare ones were on a rack by the door. Her own stupid pudding doormat face stared out at her from nearly every front page, sometimes in colour. And Daddy's face. The police had certainly been thorough. The police had really gone to town. It made her feel naked, even inside her disguise.

She picked out an *Independent*, resisting the temptation to buy half a dozen papers.

A woman passed her going out, without a glance. She was stuffing a book of stamps into her purse.

Stamps. A sense of terrible urgency seized Lucy. The

police were on the hunt, and the envelopes upstairs in her bedroom had no stamps on them. They were useless, helpless, without stamps. She turned to the sub-post office counter without thinking, and asked for twelve books of first-class stamps. That should get the envelopes *anywhere*.

Mr Patel was serving. 'Good morning, Miss Kingsmith. My, what a lot of letters you are going to be writing! Or are you merely posting early for Christmas?' His face split in a friendly grin.

But she could have screamed. She had done something monumentally stupid. She had drawn attention to herself. And now he had asked a question which she had to find an answer to. Or she would draw attention to herself more.

'Advertising,' she gasped; forcing a smile, which was not too difficult, because she liked him so much. 'I'm sending out . . . brochures . . . for the shop.'

'Advertising. Very wise,' said Mr Patel. 'It pays to advertise, when you sell beautiful things like you do. How is *my* lovely clock this morning?' There wasn't a trace of suspicion on his face.

'Fine,' she said. 'Going like a bomb.'

He nodded, smiled again. Then frowned. 'One thing concerns me about these stamps you are buying. Would it not be more economical to send by second-class post such things as brochures?'

'I want them to *get* there,' said Lucy quickly. 'I had a second-class letter yesterday that had been posted two weeks ago.'

'It is sadly true,' said Mr Patel, 'that the GPO is no longer the great British institution it once was.'

She paid Mr Patel, and walked back proud and tall, making herself nod and smile at people, and even stop to admire someone's baby in a pram. It was amazing, the way you could put on a smiling shell, even when you were a

137

panicking pulp inside. She felt Mummy would have been proud of her.

Maybe this was what growing up was all about.

The Independent had put the story into longer words, but gave no more details. It had the story on an inside page, unlike the tabloids.

As she slowly grew calmer, she thought the authorities had been very, *very* clever. They had got the whole nation looking for a murderer without actually saying he *was* a murderer. And they had set off a man-hunt without having to mention missing government documents. They had covered up the Real Fuss with False Fuss, and they had given the nation of tabloid readers what it loved. Sex and death, and evil in high places. And it gave them an excuse to drag in her photo, so that people might spot her, too. Maybe they thought that Daddy was already on his way to her; that if they found Lucy they would find Daddy as well.

The worst shock was that she had totally underestimated the enemy. Had listened all her life to Mummy and Daddy gossiping about goings-on in Whitehall. The junior Whitehall staff who chattered all day when they should be working; high-up alcoholics whose colleagues covered up for them; shocking womanizers who could hardly raise their heads before lunchtime; men in their fifties who had given up and were just sitting on their backsides waiting for their pension.

In Daddy's eyes, Government was a creaking shambles, always dropping clangers, on the verge of collapse . . . And the Cabinet, always getting everything wrong, according to the endless whingeing of the Opposition. These Cabinet ministers, grotesque and childish and pitiable on *Spitting Image* . . . But frightened governments were not like that.

Frightened governments did dreadful things and got clean away with it. Look at the French, blowing up the *Rainbow Warrior* and murdering that photographer aboard. Why had no French cabinet minister been tried for murder? Why had everyone conveniently forgotten about it?

It was as if people couldn't afford to remember . . . Trust your government or lose your sanity . . .

She was up against minds far more cunning than her own. It was like playing chess against Daddy when she was younger. She would think she had the whole game under control and then he would make one move and the whole world turned upside down.

The whole world turned upside down. She hugged herself and rocked for comfort. The power of the Government filled the shop, making her feel cold. That photograph of Daddy had been so good . . . maybe they would put it on *Crimewatch*. People who had their photographs on *Crimewatch* were often caught within minutes . . . in pubs and hotels. Three days' growth of beard wouldn't be enough to hide him. Daddy . . . Daddy . . .

And yet a little part of herself refused to be beaten. Like when she'd played Daddy at chess. There must be a way out, there must be a way to ruin their game.

And as she rocked and hugged herself, and feared someone would come in off the street to buy something, and she wouldn't be able to cope . . . suddenly it came to her.

Mr Betts.

Mr Betts knew she wasn't dead or murdered. He would tell people. It would be all right.

Oh, God, no it wouldn't. Mr Betts would tell them she'd been crying over the phone, wretched, scared. That wouldn't stop the man-hunt. It would make it worse.

But suppose she rang up Mr Betts again? Told him she was fine . . . ?

She was dialling his number when another thought hit her. Suppose he'd been to the police already? Suppose they were at his house now? *Waiting* for her to ring again? Couldn't the police trace calls?

If she was going to ring up Mr Betts, she'd better do it from a long way away.

She leapt up and checked her purse for coins for the phone. Plenty.

She swept into June's shop. 'Will you watch the shop for me? I'm going buying again. I'm *determined* to get something today.'

June stared at her. 'All right. If that's the way you feel.'

'What do you mean, if that's the way I feel?' She had to stop herself shouting at June.

'Oh . . . your money's burning a hole in your pocket. It's written all over your face. Go and get it out of your system. It's all right for some.'

There was a red phone-box at a crossroads on the high moors, with only a pub for company. The landlady was just opening up, yawning, putting out milk bottles, talking to her cat. No danger of impatient people banging on the phone-box door here. And she had put fifty miles behind her, in less than an hour.

She dialled the number and waited, playing with the tower of coins she had built by the phone. It was a woman's voice that answered.

'My husband isn't in. He went off early to the British Library. I don't expect him back till four. He's always back by four, to have a cup of tea with me.' Then her voice grew excited, avid. 'Are you one of the girls from school? Have you seen the papers? Isn't it awful about Lucy Smith? My husband taught her; he'll be heartbroken when he hears. He was just talking to her the other night . . . Did you know her?'

Lucy kept her voice low and smooth, amazed at her own skill.

'I've seen her round school. She was two years older than me.'

'Poor little thing . . . What did you say your name was?'

'Sandra Shaw,' said Lucy, wildly off the top of her head. There was nobody in school called that.

'Sandy Shaw?' asked the woman, amazed. 'You mean like the pop-star?'

'*Sandra*,' Lucy bellowed. How could Mr Betts have married such a stupid woman? '*Sandra* Shaw. Tell him I'll ring back at four, and it's *urgent*.'

'Oh, it always is, with you young ones. You think the world revolves round you. You'd think you'd let him have some peace in his holidays.'

Lucy came out of the phone-booth with five hours to kill in a totally strange place. There was only one way to stay sane. Rachel Kingsmith, dealer, was going to buy buy buy. June would not be disappointed this time.

She was back at the same phone-booth smack on four, in spite of getting lost twice, which had thrown her into a panic and made her hands slippery on the wheel. The back of the Metro was so full of good stuff the last dealer had had to tie down her tailgate with an obliging piece of old rope. The sight of all the lovely new things warmed her a little as she re-dialled the number. She was getting *efficient*.

His voice answered, solid and warm and comforting.

'Lucy? Thank God! It's you. It's really you. I've been out of my mind, worrying about you. What's all this stuff about you in the *Evening Standard*? I was just going to ring the police.'

'It's rubbish. I'm well. I'm fine.'

'But what's all this stuff about your father? Is he with you? Can I speak to him?'

'He's not here. I don't know where he is. I'm on my own. But he's OK too.'

'Then what are the police going on about? There's a full-scale search going on. What a waste of police time! We'd better let them know, straightaway. Where are you?'

She did not know what to say to him.

'Lucy? Lucy? Are you still there?'

She would always remember that moment; the pub across the road, with the faint sound of canned music coming through its open windows. In bitter memory, somehow, the tune was always Sinatra's 'My Way'.

She took a deep breath and said, 'Daddy took some papers from the Department. The Government are doing something very wicked and he's going to blow the whistle on them. He's . . . on the run. They're trying to catch him and get the evidence back. They want to hush it up.'

His voice sounded incredulous. 'Lucy, are you *sure*?'

'Positive. I've seen some of the evidence. They're faking figures about international whale-stocks. But it's more than that, much more. He said when the world found out, everyone would hate us.'

He was silent for a moment; when he came back, he sounded . . . weary. 'Lucy, I'm a bit out of my depth about this. What can I do to help?'

'Just tell the police I've rung you, and I'm alive. And well.'

'Well, I'll certainly do that.' He sounded relieved. 'All this other stuff's a bit over my head . . .'

'Don't mention it. Forget I ever said it.' Her voice was

urgent now; had she begun to fear for him, even at that point?

'Well . . . take care, Lucy . . . Keep in touch . . . when you can. I can let you know how I got on . . .' Already, his mind was elsewhere, weighing up what to do. Shrewd bloke, old Bettsy.

She rang off and drove home.

June was thrilled to bits with her stuff. Though Lucy had to knock a bit off the prices she'd paid, fearing June would think her a fool.

June bought a battered pewter tankard with a lid from her, for her Sammy's birthday. It gave Lucy exactly fifty pence profit.

She was to remember that sadly as the only lasting profit on the day.

She watched the nine o'clock news on the BBC and the ten o'clock news on ITV. But there was nothing new. The item still featured her own pudding-face and Daddy's face. There was video-footage of policemen digging in the back garden at home, searching woods and fields in long lines, with sticks and dogs. If anything, they were making *more* of it.

What on earth had happened to Bettsy? She was used to him making things happen, putting things right, *fast*. Then she remembered he wasn't in school now; he wasn't a big fish in a little pond. In the outside world, he'd be very small beer. It would take him a long time to get noticed, to make them listen. They would try to make out he was just some crackpot schoolteacher. She felt sorry for anybody who tried that one on him; he had a ferocious temper when roused.

She went to bed with her radio on Radio Two. No change on the midnight news. She dozed through 'Jazz Parade'. Jolted awake for the half-past twelve headlines. All through

'Night-ride' she dozed, jolting awake for news headlines. Nothing. What could be taking them so long? Perhaps the news department at the BBC shut down at a certain hour, and the newsreaders would go on reading the same piffling things, even if the End of the World had happened meantime . . .?

On that thought, she really slept.

By the time the next day's lunchtime news on BBC had passed with no change (except some smug Scotland Yard detective superintendent asking anyone who might have seen this girl to ring in) she began to be really afraid for Bettsy. Had he let slip that stuff about the whales? Had they arrested him on a charge of conspiracy?

The hours till the evening, when she could ring Bettsy again, dragged endlessly. She behaved like a total fool in the shop, said things were mahogany when they were clearly oak, gave the wrong change. A lot of people came into the shop, because it was Saturday. They seemed to her nothing but a nuisance. But the more off-hand and cross she got, the more they seemed to want to buy things. It was crazy, but that day she sold a chest of drawers, a hallstand, a brass coal-scuttle and her butter-tubs, three horse-brasses and a silver milk-jug. As June said, her best day ever.

But five o'clock came at last, and she could lock up and drive off across the moors with only the sheep for company.

She made herself drive to the same phone-box. Parked the car and walked across with a dreadful sinking feeling that was worse than waiting to get your GCSE results.

The number was engaged. In a rage, she re-dialled immediately; over and over again; as if she could force the line open with the power of her mind. After ten minutes, she went for an agitated walk. Came back and tried again.

Engaged, engaged, engaged, engaged. She rang the operator and asked her to test for a fault on the line. The operator came back and said the line was working normally, just busy.

Another walk. She tried again. Engaged.

Some lads sitting outside the pub drinking began to notice her – point and laugh. They obviously thought she was a jilted lover, stood-up by her boyfriend. One of them came drifting across, weighed her up, and offered her a drink. To drown her sorrows, he said. That finally drove her away.

After that, it was just a nightmare of driving anywhere, and ringing from every phone-box she saw. And all the time her fear grew. *Who* could be phoning the Bettses this much?

It was dusk before she finally got through, in some little village whose name she never knew.

It wasn't him. It was a young man's voice. She almost dropped the phone, fearing it was a policeman's voice. But there was a weariness about it, a dreariness, that could not possibly belong to a policeman.

'Could I speak to Mr Betts, please?'

'Speaking.'

Was she going mad?

'I mean – the older Mr Betts.'

There was a long and dreadful silence, then the voice at the far end swallowed and said, 'I'm afraid my father died last night.'

'*Died?*' Her voice went up in a shriek.

His voice went on, wearily, patiently. She could recognize the flatness of bereavement now; from when Mummy died.

'He had a heart attack, they think. He had a phone-call from some girl at school, and told my mother he was going out to sort something out. My mother thought nothing of it; he was always doing that sort of thing. But he rang back shortly after, saying he was helping the police with the Lucy

145

Smith enquiry, and was going with them somewhere by car, and not to wait dinner for him.

'We were still waiting up for him at midnight when two police came to the door – a man and a woman. He'd had a heart attack, they said, at some place in Sussex, and been rushed to Horsham General Hospital but was dead on arrival. There's going to have to be a post-mortem. We've no idea when the funeral is going to be. Are you one of the girls from school . . . ?'

'Ye . . . es. Yes.'

'Which one were you?'

Even as the world collapsed about her, she kept her head; just.

'Claire Bassett.'

'Oh, yes, I've heard him speak of you. He was very fond of you. He said you were very good at tennis.'

Could she, even now, feel a twinge of jealousy?

'He was a wonderful man,' she said. 'Everybody loved him.'

'I know. People have been ringing up all day. People have been wonderful. The phone's never stopped . . .'

How close to him she felt. How utterly weary he sounded, poor young man. Yet she wanted to keep on talking to him, keep him close, not let him go. He was the nearest she'd ever get again, to Bettsy.

'How old was he?'

'Only fifty. He never ailed a thing. Seemed as fit as a fiddle. Nobody in our family's ever died of a heart attack. My grandfather's still going strong at eighty . . . Dad rode his bike everywhere, played squash, never ate butter or salt. He smoked his pipe, but not all that much. He fiddled with it more than he smoked it.' What came through was his terrible sense of unfairness. But death was always unfair . . .

146

'Dad was always helping people. He never turned anybody away. He just couldn't say no. I suppose that's what killed him.'

At the far end of the phone, she heard a smothered yawn. Even when you were bereaved, you still got tired.

'Thank you very much,' she said, suddenly sounding too formal, as if somebody had offered her a tray of drinks at a party.

'Are you coming to his funeral? Everyone seems to be coming.' He sounded almost eager now; that strange eagerness of bereavement.

'I'll try,' she said. Too shrilly; for that was a terrifying thought. 'Goodnight. Tell your mother how sorry I am.'

Then she hung up. And saw with amazement that only two coins remained of the tower she had built by the phone. She had fed the rest in, without even realizing.

She had killed him. But for her, he'd be sitting by his own fireside now, talking to his wife, laughing with his son, watching the telly.

She had used him like a pawn; and like a pawn, he had been swept from the board. She had sent him roaring off, avid to right a wrong, put straight an injustice, as he had done a hundred times before. Only, this time, into a deadly world he must never have understood.

But *she* had understood it.

Had they tried to frighten him into silence? Shut his mouth with threats? If so, they hadn't known her Bettsy . . .

Or had they just decided he knew too much, like Hilda Murrell? Nodded to each other, behind his unsuspecting back? Poor Bettsy, who believed too much in decency and justice, who thought all men were as decent as he was.

She writhed; she rocked to and fro. She had not guessed

147

the world could contain so much agony. She pressed her face against the cool glass of the phone-box and stared across the dusky street to where lighted windows showed people watching the flicker of telly, or sitting eating, or just standing talking. They seemed to her a million miles away, as strange as Martians in their painless innocence.

She might have writhed for ever, if a new thought hadn't hit her. It was so easy to murder, if you were the State; held the police, the coroner, the judge and jury in the palm of your hand. They would have ways of murdering that even a pathologist wouldn't find in a post-mortem, even if the pathologist wasn't their own man and . . .

If they had killed Bettsy, who knew so little . . .

They would kill her too. It would be so easy. Already, on the newscasts, she was a murder victim. Dead already. Daddy would get the blame.

And Daddy? When they caught him? Easy enough to fake a suicide. Lots of murderers committed suicide afterwards, racked with remorse. Happened every week . . . She remembered that official phrase in *The Independent*: 'A double fatality is not ruled out.'

Easy. There was nothing to stop them. No way out.

Except . . . the State itself might die. And the magic bullets that could kill even a State . . . ?

A pile of jiffy-bags lying on her dressing-table at home.

The icy fear inside her seemed to . . . set hard. This was the way it was meant to happen. The logic was inexorable. The State had killed Bettsy. The State was a mad wild beast. No one was safe. The State must die. Nothing else mattered now. She refused to live in the same world as this State.

But now she must be very calm, very cool, very careful. Until the bullets were fired, until the packets were well on their way. After that, nothing much mattered.

She drove home, very careful not to exceed the speed

limit. Before she reached home, she filled up the car with petrol.

She drove past her own front door. There was nobody about, except the usual crowd of youths and girls round the lighted chippy, quarter of a mile further on. Only the usual cars were parked, and Mr Patel's van. She knew them all by heart. Her curtains upstairs were not drawn, and the cats were sitting on the upstairs windowsill, watching for her and whiling away the time washing themselves. They wouldn't be that relaxed and bored if there were strangers in the house. All the other houses had windows lit which were always lit; all had curtains drawn, with no cracks where someone might be watching.

She parked, went in. The house was cold, undisturbed. The jiffy-bags were where she had left them, ready-addressed, with the stamps stuck on correctly, a pound's worth for the Common Market, four pounds' worth for Air Mail.

She fed the cats, to stop them twining round her legs, trampling on her desk as she wrote. They came and sat around her, washing again in contentment, as she wrote the same note neatly, over and over. There was no longer any point in disguising her writing . . .

Dear Sir,
    The British Government is doing something very evil.
The details are in this envelope. They are faking the
figures for whale-stocks. I don't know what else they are
doing but it is very bad. Yours sincerely
Lucy Smith

It sounded so weak and feeble. But it was the best she could do. She read one note for a last time, and sealed up the jiffies, and put them into a carrier bag marked: 'The Village Shop. Proprietor K. V. Patel. Patel's for Value.'

Then she put out the downstairs lights, and, after ten minutes, her bedroom light, as if she was going to sleep. Then she came out of the shop door in a silent rush, bag over one arm, shop keys in one hand, car keys in the other. She shot off up the street like a rocket. By this time, only Mr Patel's upstairs light was still on, for it was near midnight. Mr Patel, doing his books, burning the midnight oil? Be safe, Mr Patel. Prosper. Go on believing in Britain, while you can.

She watched in her driving-mirror. No car pulled out to follow her. Not a soul moved in the battered little street, under the street-lamps.

She parked at her old favourite parking space, at the head of the valley. Where she had sat by the stream in despair, the day she had first gone to June's shop. What had *that* girl had to despair over? Silly foolish innocent doormat Lucy Smith?

Now, her eyes searched the whole moonlit valley. Her dash for freedom should have flushed them out . . .

But nothing stirred.

Her eyes searched the prettily clouded sky for the lights of a helicopter; her ears cocked for the blatt of its rotors. She kept it up for ten minutes, shivering a little as the night breeze touched her.

Nothing. She was clean away; unless some hidden watcher had radioed ahead.

But the watcher wouldn't know about Five Lane Ends, just beyond where she had parked. A crossroads out of which five roads led. Little twisting moorland roads, little more than gated tracks. But the signposts carried grand big names like Manchester, Leeds, Huddersfield, Carlisle. It was a local joke, a *very* local joke.

But not a joke tonight. The five lanes forked, became twenty-five, then fifty. Leading into every part of Lancashire, Yorkshire, Cumbria.

They couldn't watch them all.

The moonlight was so strong, she could drive without lights. She didn't put her headlights on till she met the first massive innocent juggernaut, climbing its slow way out of Huddersfield. Nothing followed; nothing was waiting for her; nothing, in her rear-view mirror, put on its lights and started up.

She dropped the first jiffy at a little sub-post office on the road to Leeds.

The rest of the night was a maze, as she cut back and forth across northern England. Sometimes she was on the open moor, between high stone walls, where the red glinting eyes of foxes and rabbits were her only company, or the green glint of a hunting cat. Once she saw, under her headlights, a tiny mouse running across the road for dear life, travelling so fast it appeared to be running on its hindlegs alone. She was so glad it made it to the verge, though she'd been too amazed at the sight to brake. At other times, she was in the vast lighted emptiness of city centres, where the traffic-lights changed from red to green for nobody but her. She remembered afterwards posting one jiffy under the bulk of York Minister . . . The main post office of Darlington; a solitary post-box in Jesmond, a posh suburb of Newcastle.

All her fear had gone; most of the time she lived in the visual wonder of the world she might soon be leaving. At other times, she wondered about heroes. Her old heroes were no use to her any more. Not even the Duke of Wellington, with his elegant jokes, made under fire. Not even poor Lord Nelson. Establishment dupes, every one. She groped for a different kind of hero in her memory now. Wat Tyler in the Peasant's Revolt. Stabbed in the back treacherously, by the

151

Lord Mayor of London. John Ball, the hedge-priest. Executed. Jack Cade. The mutineers at the Nore; hanged from the yard-arm. All come to a bad end, for defying the State. And so few. Or were the rest forgotten, their names wiped out? Her mind even drifted abroad. Ulrike Meinhof, terrorist. But such a gentle loving face, from her photographs . . .

Still, they kept her company. A goodly company, though small.

The last jiffy thudded down into the box in the silent main street of Kirby Stephen.

And then she was driving home, with the sun coming up in glory over the moors, and the needle of her petrol gauge trembling over her last half-gallon.

It was finished, done. And she felt very far from this world, but oddly content. She thought of salmon that journey thousands of miles, than spawn and die; of plants that spread their seeds and wither. Whatever happened now, she had done all she could. There was peace, in which she could weep for Mr Betts. She had to stop driving several times, to wipe her eyes, when she could no longer see to drive.

And so she came home; it seemed so precious, all of a sudden. The polished chairs in her shop window; the slowly moving pendulum of the grandfather clock, showing like a wink through its little window. A bottle of milk waiting on the step, and the whirr of the milk float as it passed her, returning.

It was the usual milkman; he gave her a wave and a smile, and she waved and smiled back.

She crept into bed by the black phone. And slept, and woke to weep for Bettsy. And slept again.

The phone stayed silent.

Chapter Fifteen

'Nowt in the paper as usual,' announced June five mornings later. 'Nowt but that young girl who's still missing. Never known them make such a fuss. Not even about that Suzy Lamplugh, the estate-agent girl. Silly season – everybody on holiday and nowt happening.' She tossed the paper down and said, 'Even me horoscope's up the creek. It's supposed to be a bad time for me financially, and yet they're buying every bit of rubbish I've got in the shop. Even that mezzotint of W. E. Gladstone's gone. I quite miss the vinegary old sod – I must've had him five years.'

Lucy picked up the paper. They really were making a fuss, though there wasn't a single new thing to report. Except a twist she'd bitterly expected. Some police spokesman had said there were now fears for the life of the father, as well as the daughter . . .

June came back with two mugs, making her jump. 'You know, they had that girl on *Crimewatch* last Monday. That's not usual. Most of them *Crimewatch* cases are ancient ones the police have given up on. Real no-hopers. Makes you wonder what's behind it.' She gave her coffee an extra stir, with a solitary bent fork of classical design, that lurked on her desk. 'You know, that girl's face *haunts* me. I keep on feeling I've seen her before somewhere . . . Mebbe it's only seeing it in the paper so often.'

'Let's have a go with that fork,' said Lucy, taking it off her.

'I put your usual in,' said June. 'I don't think that modern sugar dissolves the way it used to. They're always mucking about with things, but nobody'll ever tell *us*.'

Yes, thought Lucy. They're not getting anywhere, and they're getting desperate. And where are those jiffy-bags now? They must all have arrived, yet . . . nothing. She had a nasty vision again, of the jiffies landing in waste-paper baskets . . . and then her calm returned.

She had been curiously happy, these last four days, living in a sort of cocoon, an invisible bubble that enclosed only her shop and the small life of the village. Every day the sun had shone, bringing people into the shop in a buying mood. In four days, she had made three hundred pounds profit. Enough to pay the rent, buy petrol for the car, put something towards the phone and electric bills, and even buy food. June told her, with great seriousness, that she was getting *known*. Maybe, she thought, dreamily, sometimes, just maybe, nothing was ever going to come in from the outside again, and she would live and die here, Rachel Kingsmith, antique-dealer, successful in a tiny way.

Daddy! But even the memory of Daddy was starting to blur round the edges . . . Maybe he too would escape for good and vanish and never appear in her life again. Or else turn up and share her safe place, and they could live a harmless humdrum existence together. This sunny morning, it no longer seemed impossible.

Then her shop window darkened, and she flinched and knew how shallow her surface happiness was, and how deep her terrors.

'S'only Trev,' said June. 'Hope he's got something tasty on board . . .'

But Trev was in a holiday mood, elegantly turned out in a straw boater and pink striped blazer, and looking less like Trotsky than some young Cambridge friend of Lewis Carroll. He grinned broadly, and said, 'I've come to take you to *Chelford*, Rachel.'

'Oh, you *lucky* girl,' said June, her little face lighting up wistfully. 'Chelford's lovely. I wish I could come, but someone's got to watch the shop.'

'But . . .' said Lucy.

'Go on,' said June. 'I *insist*. You can't miss *Chelford*.'

And at the first sign of Lucy's resistance, Trev's face had fallen so. She couldn't bear to wipe away that look of happiness. Happiness was so frail and precious. They were her good and loving friends. And Daddy had said he would only ring up in the evenings . . .

'If you miss Chelford,' said June, 'you'll always regret it. I still remember the first time I went. My father took me. I was only a young girl then; I hadn't really started.'

'But . . . if the phone goes . . .?'

'I'll take it,' said June reassuringly. 'I'll sit in your shop today, and pretend I'm a posh lady dealer. Go on, enjoy yourself.'

'You'll write down any messages? Have a pad and pencil ready?'

'Who you expectin'? Sotheby's? Or the John Paul Getty Museum?' June's face was suddenly sharper, curious. Then she laughed and said, 'Get off wi' you. Wear your best frock. You could do wi' a nice day out. You look peaky. You've been working too hard.'

She let herself be swept away by her two good friends. And even in her terrible last hours, she could not bring herself to regret it.

They settled comfortably together, as the massive pick-up roared and rattled its way down the valley

'What is this Chelford, then? Kingdom of Heaven?'

Trev stabbed her a blue-eyed grin. 'Country auction. In the village hall. The last real country auction the big dealers haven't found. Whole housefuls of stuff – anything might turn up. Everyone sits around on the furniture – even the village copper. And the home-made sandwiches are out of this world. If I was dead, and allowed back to earth one day a year as a ghost, I'd come to Chelford auction.'

She felt close to the heart of him; closer than she'd ever hoped to get. So she said, 'I like riding in your pick-up,' because she knew that was close to the heart of him too.

'Designed her nearly all meself. It's a Dodge, but it's got a Ford V8 engine, disc-brakes all round, racing suspension, extra-strong shockers. She's done a hundred and thirty up the motorway. Coming back from Birmingham Flea-market at six in the morning, wi' an oak sideboard on the back.'

She made the right admiring noises. 'You've got a lot of spotlights and radios . . .'

'Just flash, really. Showing off. Gives me a sense of power, after a day at Social Security. And after a day at Social Security, by God I need it. I park it next to the manager's Granada – doesn't half make him mad. That's a CB radio there. Like to try it?' Then he added hurriedly, 'Get a lot of truckers – their language can get a bit rough. Why spoil a lovely day?'

She left it, because she didn't want to spoil the lovely day. The windows were down, and as they crossed the Mersey into green Cheshire, the smells of harvest and fruitfulness crept in past the motorway smell of burnt hydrocarbons.

'This truck's my girlfriend really, I suppose. I spoil her something rotten. Nothing but the best. Hang around Halford's wondering what to buy her for Christmas. The windscreen's Perspex, bullet-proof. Like they had in Spitfires in the war. Mate did it for me.'

She nearly laughed out loud. 'Why bullet-proof?'

'Well, can't be broken by flying stones.' Then he added, 'I suppose it's fantasy really. Sometimes on long drives I pretend she's a Spitfire. Or the Starship Enterprise. I'm just a big kid really. I don't want to grow up.'

'Suits me,' she said, wriggling her bottom to make herself even more comfortable. This whole day was unreal. But lovely.

'She's better than a woman. I mean, when she gets awkward, I can fix *her*.'

'Do you think all women are more awkward than men?'

'God, yes. The only things men care about are cars, hobbies and booze. You know where you are with them. I mean, every time me dad has a birthday, I buy him six ounces of Player's Rough-cut Shag. He knows it's coming, he's as happy as anything. Saves him buying any for six weeks.

'But me mother . . . every birthday's a nightmare. She says how lovely, then puts what you've bought her away in a cupboard an' you never see it again. I gave her a bronze of the goddess Kali the Destroyer last year, and she wouldn't even *touch* it. And when I went to Australia I brought her back a bit of Ayers Rock . . . all polished up beautifully. And she asked what it was *for*!'

Lucy kept her face straight. All the way to Chelford. And there it was. Chelford village hall, planks painted a dark tasteful green. Piled up outside, stone urns thick with moss, eight battered lawn-mowers, a hen-hut on cast-iron wheels, a life-size classical statue with only one arm, and a row of leaning 1930s hat-stands.

'That's just the outside stuff,' said Trev. 'Wait till you see the inside.'

The inside was a mass of farm-hands and wives, already lolling on 1930s three-piece suites; squatting on bulbous-legged tables like groups of roosting hens, taking occasional pecks at six-packs of lager scattered around. The walls were a tangle of hayforks and black bicycles, scythes and Bendix washing-machines with sagging doors, oil-paintings of litters of pigs and nests of brass pans black with age.

But it was the bed Lucy fell for. Headboard and footboard nearly seven feet across, a mass of gleaming dark red mahogany, of turned pillars, elaborate bobbles, carved bearded faces and Gothic arches. The footboard was only four feet tall, but the headboard was six. A Victorian masterpiece that must weigh a ton . . .

'You'll never sell that,' said Trev. 'People would be terrified of it. Imagine that in an ordinary semi. You'd think it was leaping off the wall at you, like Jack the Ripper. You'd need a stately home.'

'But it's beautiful. I want it . . . for *me*!'

'It won't go in my pick-up. You'd belt lumps off passing cars.'

'I don't care. I *love* it!'

Trev gave her a dire look; she had joined his mother in the ranks of impossible women.

The young auctioneer tapped his microphone. 'Can we have a little quiet, ladies and gentlemen?' Then, 'Lot one – a noble pair of stone lions. Put them on your gateposts to sneer at the passing peasants. Who'll start me at twenty-five? Twenty, then? Fifteen? They don't need much feeding – only a tin of Whiskas occasionally . . .'

It was fun. Everyone knew everyone. People made bids by waving half-eaten sandwiches in the air. The porter, who displayed the items, was a complete comedian; modelling the feathered lady's hats on his own head, doing a catwalk strut in a moth-eaten fur coat, even wrapping an ancient pink corset round his ample chest and giving a sexy wiggle.

'Thank you, Harry,' the auctioneer would say, as the laughing died down. 'Harry's appearing in the lead role of *Call Me Madam* at the Stockport Palladium next month . . .'

Or some such crack. But the pair of them were no fools really. People laughed, and, in a good humour, bid up good prices for real rubbish.

The village policeman, huge in his uniform, got a pair of brass candlesticks for twenty-five, and took them into custody there and then.

'Ain't yer got no electric light down at the nick, Ted? More Government cuts?'

Through the long sunny day, they sat and bid. There was no break for lunch. Trev slid away for sandwiches; as a gesture of contempt, while the endless Toby-jugs were being auctioned. They indeed proved heavenly sandwiches. Newly baked bread with thick crumbling slabs of home-cooked ham in between. And then some home-baked meringues, thick with clotted cream.

Is this all real? wondered Lucy. Or am I dreaming? This is not the way the world is. Or am I dead and in heaven already? But the dream persisted, through five hundred lots, and her soul and body insisted on enjoying it. She bid with authority now. Got a solid brass fender for thirty, and an Art Nouveau fireside companion for twenty.

'People don't like Art Noove up here, yet,' muttered Trev. 'They don't want what their auntie had in her house, they want what their granny had. But you'll get a good price for them, down south.'

Finally, they came to lot 497, the huge bed.

'How would you get it home?' hissed Trev. 'They haven't got a delivery service, you know. People just take their own stuff when they leave.'

'I'll get Big Artie.'

'He'll *bankrupt* you. You won't get it up the stairs. Still, you'll get it for nowt. You'll be the only bidder, you see.'

But there *was* a rival bidder. A little man in a dirty grey cap in the front row.

'Hell! *Him!*' Trev was positively snarling. 'Johnson. He buys good old stuff and cuts it up, and makes crappy new things with it. A *faker*! He's a *menace. Stop* him, Rachel!'

He even clutched her arm in his excitement.

Up and up the bidding went. The room fell silent, awed. People sat transfixed with sandwiches halfway to their mouths, when they saw something they wouldn't give tuppence for climbing up into the hundreds. Then came the whispers.

'They say she's a London dealer.'

'More likely one of them big shippers out of Lancashire.'

'Hope she beats the little bastard.'

Two hundred. Three hundred. Four hundred. Five.

But Lucy was beyond sense. The horrid little man would *not* cut up her lovely thing. And Trev was still gripping her arm, tight as a clam. Trev, who preferred things to women . . .

At six hundred, the little man faltered, doing sums softly with resentfully moving lips.

'The bidding is against you, sir!'

The little man shook his head so violently, Lucy was afraid it might drop off.

'Going, then, at six hundred. Going, going, gone.'

The gavel banged; there was tremendous applause for Lucy. The little man stopped in front of her, tore up his bidding card and threw it at her feet. Then stamped out.

'I'll have a word with Big Artie,' said Trev. 'Well done, Rachel!'

It was nearly the last item. When the auctioneer had finished a crowd gathered round the bed, yawning and stretching, but avidly interested.

'That Johnson . . . I never thought he'd go a tenth as high.'

'Damn near bankrupted himself. He hasn't got two pennies to rub together.'

160

'He knows his furniture though. He must have spotted *something*.'

'Tom here thinks it might have come from Astley Hall. Lord Astley's own bed.'

'I reckon it's not Victorian. I reckon it's Regency Gothick. God knows what it would fetch at Sotheby's. Thousands, I reckon.'

'Regency Gothick's the coming thing. Very collectable . . .'

Lucy and Trev stood silently listening, while the crowd, who'd thought nothing of the bed, went into wilder and wilder fantasies about it.

Finally, the thin man who had said Regency Gothick was very collectable, sidled across to her.

'*Is* it Regency Gothick, madam?'

'Could be,' said Trev, enthusiastically.

A slightly false enthusiasm, Lucy thought. So she just said, 'I don't know. I just love it.'

The thin man surveyed her shrewdly. 'You wouldn't take eight hundred for it? Two hundred instant profit, and no delivery charges? You won't even have to write a cheque – I'll do that. And I'll give you the two hundred in notes . . .'

'No tax,' muttered Trev. 'No VAT. Two hundred for nowt, for lifting your hand . . .'

'No,' said Lucy. 'I said. I love it.'

'Nine hundred then?' asked the thin man. He got out a very thick wad of notes. 'Nine-fifty then? My final offer . . .'

Lucy still shook her head. But the more she shook her head, the more eager the thin man became, licking his thin lips nervously.

'All right, madam, *eleven* hundred?'

No.

'Twelve hundred then?'

'That's a *very* handsome offer,' said Trev, thoughtfully.

161

Lucy thought it was, too. Six hundred pounds, just for raising her hand to an auctioneer . . . nothing to pay Big Artie . . . no hassle getting it upstairs. Her mind swayed to and fro, like a seesaw.

How could she have ever guessed that that seesaw was swaying between her own future life and her own future death? She only looked again at the luscious gleam of the red mahogany, at the superb carving of the heads and said, 'No. I love it too much. But if I ever sell it, you can have first refusal.'

She smiled tentatively at the man, afraid she was offending him. But he smiled back at her, and said, 'Fair enough. Here's my card.'

A nice man. They shook hands. Then she and Trev went to pay for the things they'd bought.

All the way home, Trev kept raving about the bed he had once so despised. How it would amaze Flora, and what Jessie would say when she saw it. Ken would know if it was Regency Gothick. Ken went to the really big auctions, and knew all about Regency Gothick. It was a *serious* bed . . .

He sounded as if he was going to rouse the whole country to admire it. The telephone wires would be hot tonight . . . his enthusiasm was very touching. It would be nice if he would grab her by the arm again. Or even hold her hand . . .

But he didn't. His mind was all on the *thing*.

She didn't really mind. It was the end of a lovely day, and she was tired. She dozed off in the sun, with the warm sweet air beating on her face through the open window.

Chapter Sixteen

The endless ringing of the telephone dragged her up out of her dream. At first a little resentfully, for it was the nicest possible dream; driving with Trev and this time he *was* holding her hand. Then, in a great panic . . .

She held the wrong end of the phone to her ear and heard, from the other end, far away, the squawk that could only be Daddy.

'Kitten, kitten, are you there?'

She reversed the phone awkwardly, wrestling it with both hands, so the flex wrapped round her wrist.

'Daddy, you all right?'

'Just about.' He sounded grim. 'Look, kitten, can you pick me up? I'm rather a long way away, but I'm *stuck*.'

'Where? Where, Daddy?'

'Newport Pagnell service station, on the M1. Southbound side. It's south of Rugby.'

'Why – how – are you stuck?' She was wide awake now, quiveringly awake.

'They're checking all the northbound traffic, kitten. I don't know why they're watching northbound and not the southbound, but they are. I had to nip across the bridge quick, or they'd have had me. They don't seem to be checking the southbound at all.'

She shut her eyes in agony. She knew why they were checking the northbound stuff. Because she'd told Bettsy

163

she was in the north. They must have got that out of Bettsy, before they killed him.

'Kitten, kitten, are you there?' His voice sounded quite desperate; she thought he kept swallowing. 'Kitten, I hate to drag you into this. But it's the middle of the night and it's pouring outside, and I can't find anywhere to lie up and hide. Once you're soaked, people notice you. And they won't give you lifts. I only hope I can stay awake. If I fall asleep, the service station security men will pick me up – I bear a horrible resemblance to some old tramp. I haven't washed properly for days. I *stink*. Once I get dry, I'll go away again. With all this stuff. I'll leave you in the clear. I hate doing this, but it's all gone so *wrong* . . .'

'Daddy, I'm coming, I'm *coming*. Straightaway. How long will it take me?'

'About two hours, this time of night, if you put your foot down. Look, when you get here, search for me. I stick out like a sore thumb. But when you see me, don't come over to me. Just make sure I've seen you, then do something like going to the ladies or buying a bar of chocolate, then drift back to your car. What make is it?'

'Metro. Grey. E546 DMD.'

'Right. Hurry then.' His voice rose in a desperate wail, so unlike him. 'Oh, I wish it hadn't happened like this.'

'See you at Newport Pagnell,' she said firmly, and rang off.

She slipped on her warmest clothes, went to the loo and then out to the car. It wasn't raining here yet, but she could feel the odd tiny spit of wet against her cheek. The street was empty, desolate. But then it would be; it was five past two in the morning.

*

164

She had the M6 almost to herself. Under her headlights it was as empty as a tennis court. You really could've played tennis on it, if you dodged the occasional car. Often there was nothing at all in sight. She grew glad of the friendly red points of a car's tail-light, half a mile ahead. The motorway was *too* empty. So lonely. More traffic would've given her problems to take her mind off things.

But at least she could put her foot down, in any lane she chose. She clocked a steady eighty; the engine note never faltered; her tank was full. After the last time, she'd kept it that way.

If only there was more to look at. Just the ugly backs of floodlit factories, the big blue illuminated signs, the shattered bits of blown-out lorry tyres on the hard shoulder. Once a rabbit ran across, then suddenly stopped and went up on its hindlegs, as her headlight beams caught it and made it glow like a candle-flame. She steered, veered, wildly, to avoid it; but the screech of her tyres must have panicked it, for at the last moment it ducked under her wheels and she heard a sharp thud against the floor beneath her feet and, looking back in the mirror, she saw it lying on the tarmac, flattened and still. She could've wept for it, but kept her face straight and her eyes on the road. She told herself the rabbit's troubles were over . . .

She thought of Trev, and his fantasy that his pick-up was a Spitfire. Was this how the young men had felt in their Spitfires; twice as alive as usual, hearts beating a little too hard, inside a wire cage of nerves? Hurling themselves into something they couldn't see the end of . . .

Where would she be, this time tomorrow?

Well, what would happen would happen, and there was nothing she could do to stop it. She squirmed about in her seat, settling her aching bum a little more comfortably; and grasping at little fleeting straws of memories, of the wonderful day at Chelford.

Where should she park? Up with the handful of other cars, next to the lights of the service station? Or far far back in the dark?

Up with the others would be safer, less noticeable; but her mind craved the darkness like a drug. Walking up through the dark would give her time to settle her face and body . . .

She parked far back in the dark, already knowing it was a bad mistake.

The torrential rain had stopped, twenty miles back. But great pools of water on the tarmac reflected the brilliant lights of the service station, upside down. She switched off the engine, then turned the ignition on again, to check the fuel-gauge. Nearly full; she had filled up at Hylton Park. She didn't want to go anywhere near the bright lights, once she had Daddy aboard.

Then she locked the car carefully. Walked with trembling legs up the long straggling isthmuses of drying tarmac, between the long puddles. It seemed to take for ever . . .

Only once did she pause. A tiny faint burst of noise, electronic noise, far off. Tinny, like the DJ's voice on a distant transistor radio . . .

She could not think what it might be; she had never heard the noise of a walkie-talkie radio, such as policemen use.

The neon-lights were blinding, hurting, after the dark. Bright blue tubular girders; and an oddly out-of-place triangular painting of some stately home above the entrance . . . It was all lit up as in the working day, but the very air seemed to ache with the weariness of four in the morning.

166

Hardly anybody about. She felt as if the building itself was watching her. She must search but not look as if she was searching. She must seem natural, whatever was natural at four in the morning in a near-deserted motorway service station.

Well, the loo was natural. In fact, once she thought of it, imperative. She felt better, and checked her pale weary face in the mirror. Her eyes were huge; they alone would give her away, if anyone looked at her. She made herself repair her chignon, however badly her fingers trembled. And replace the lipstick she'd licked off in her tension.

Then she drifted. Into the self service café. But he wasn't there, only one family, huddled over a fretful baby. And a huge fat man reading the *Daily Mirror* with an abandoned plate of fried stuff at his elbow. She consoled herself that no man so fat could possibly be working for MI5 . . .

Then the chef emerged behind the counter, in his soiled whites, looked at her enquiringly, and she turned and walked away abruptly.

Daddy wasn't in the shop that sold sweets and tomorrow's papers either. Near panic, she got a grip on herself and bought an *Independent* and a huge bar of chocolate.

Where else was there to look?

She drifted up the stairs on to the bridge over the motorway, and watched the odd car pass below, her mind a blank. Went as far as the downward stair on the far side. Saw the legs and waterproof blue jacket of a policeman and fled before she could stop herself. The clattering of her heels seemed to fill the world. He *must* have noticed . . .

But no one followed.

Her heart was pounding. Had they caught Daddy already?

Then, at the bottom of the southbound stair, she heard a racking cough ahead. There was a man standing by the door

167

of the men's toilets. A man with a backpack and anorak and boots, a bobble-hat and dark growth of beard. He looked quite neat really; just very weary. But *was* it Daddy?

The man looked up, hearing her footsteps. And gave the slightest possible nod, such as any stranger might give, met at 4 a.m. in a motorway service station. But her heart ballooned within her, as if it would burst her whole body apart and splatter it all over these shiny unfeeling walls.

She made herself walk stiff-legged out of the entrance, and then she was dodging puddles. It was harder to see, with the light fading away behind her. She felt the water splash up her ankles. It was soothing, somehow. Refreshing. Her eyes strained ahead, watching for her car to loom up, against the dark line of bushes.

It was then she heard the noise again. The sound like a DJ's voice on a distant tranny.

She paused, listening, but it did not come a third time.

She resumed walking and then, almost drowned by the sound of her footsteps, she heard two small metallic bonks. As if someone had twice tapped the side of a car, somewhere ahead.

Again, she stopped, straining eyes and ears. She could see her car now, as her eyes got used to the dark . . .

There was someone standing beside the car. She froze up completely.

Then the someone started to move away. Unsteadily, on wobbly legs. A drunk, she thought, in wild relief. Only a drunk. As if to confirm her guess, the someone half-buried himself inside the dark bushes, still swaying unsteadily. There was the sound of pattering water, falling on fallen leaves. It was disgusting and very comforting at the same time. A drunk relieving himself.

The figure turned towards her, showing a tiny white blur of face. White patches fumbled where the flies of trousers

168

would be. Then the creature shambled off towards the dark bulk of three or four parked lorries. He went between two, and she heard a cab door slam.

Drunken lorry driver sleeping it off. Those bushes must be *stinking*!

She hurried up to her car. Remembered to unlock the tailgate for Daddy's big backpack. Then got in, and unlocked the passenger door for him. Sat and waited in the dark.

She never saw him coming, though she watched in her mirror. The first thing she knew was the tailgate going up, and a cold draught on the back of her neck. She did not turn round even when the passenger door opened, and the car sagged under the weight of his body, and she felt his knee touch hers, and smelt the over-strong smell of him. Normally it would have been offensive; but after so long without him, it was wonderful, an extra bonus. It was Daddy all right.

The car door clicked shut, quietly as a whisper. Then she turned to fling her arms round him. But he said sharply, 'No. Not here,' and her arms fell back to her sides.

'Later, kitten, later. First things first. You fit to drive back?'

'Of course.' Now she had him safe, she felt she could drive for ever.

'I'd take a spell driving. Only I keep falling asleep. It'd be too dangerous . . .'

'No problem.' She turned the key and the engine, still warm, fired first time.

'South to the next interchange,' he said. 'Nobody followed me out to the car. I *think* we're clear.'

She thought of telling him about the drunk; but it seemed pointless to worry him. A drunk was only a drunk.

No car followed them on to the southbound motorway. She looked back and the road was clear as far as she could see. At the interchange, she had a wild temptation to take to the little country roads and lose them both in the lovely dark for ever. But it would take so much longer getting him home by the little roads; they would arrive home in broad daylight, and that she didn't want.

And he was already sagging gently in sleep against her shoulder . . .

She kept on the motorway until the turn-off for home. Nothing followed; but she kept having that little nagging temptation to take to the minor roads.

It would have made no difference. Had she ever thought to look inside the rear wheel-arch on the driver's side of the Metro, she might have noticed two small round objects that had not been there before. Clinging to the scraped-clean metal like magnetic limpets.

By the aid of those two round objects, the Government helicopter, flying very low without lights and some distance off, could track them on its radio-loop all the way.

They arrived home in sunlight; but, thank heaven, empty silent sunlight. The milk was already on the doorstep. Only one pint, but she could nip down to Mr Patel's for another later. She must not *order* more; not till people knew about Daddy.

He wakened, as the car stopped.

'We here? Oh, nice shop!'

Even in her utter weariness, she flushed with pleasure. But still got out and unlocked the shop door in a hurry. The sharp tink of the shop bell was like a blessing. When she turned back for him, he was already right behind her in the doorway, backpack in his arms. She was grateful for his quickness and let him struggle past and locked the door, just as the milk float sighed past on its return journey. She didn't want *anyone* to know he was here yet. He'd need *days* to get over things; she'd have to buy him some new clothes . . .

They looked at each other, and grinned faintly in the ticking darkness of the shop.

'You look *so* like your mother, in that gear . . .'

'You look like something out of *Scott of the Antarctic* . . .'

Then they were hugging each other, really hugging each other, as if there was no tomorrow. Oh, Daddy, Daddy, Daddy . . .

And yet she was the first to break away. Both June and the postman had been known to come early.

'Would you like your breakfast in bed?'

'Just a mug of tea, kitten. And your loo. Then . . . sleep. I feel I could sleep the clock round.'

She led him upstairs, to the room she had got ready for him. Suddenly she thought it looked very thin and shabby. So it gave her a deep good feeling when he said, 'This is nice.'

She ran downstairs to put the kettle on, listening for the sounds of his feet above.

But there were none, and when she went upstairs with the tea, he was lying stretched along the bed in what he had stood up in, even his dirty anorak; dead to the world again.

She dared to take his boots off, to make him more comfortable. There were great holes in his socks; and through them showed blisters that had burst and bled. How far had he had to walk? He must have been half-crippled . . . and the smell . . .

She went and got the blankets from her own bed, and piled them on top of him. He muttered in his sleep. It might have been Mummy's name, Fiona. But otherwise he never stirred. She left the tea anyway, in case he should wake and be thirsty.

Suddenly, her own weariness hit her. To hell with the

shop today. It was too risky. Daddy might call out, half-asleep, when there were customers in; June sometimes asked to use the phone in her own bedroom, and might hear his breathing . . .

She locked the shop door, checked the sign said 'Closed', fed the cats, picked up the old blanket from her rocking-chair, threw herself fully clad on to the ruin of her own bed and was instantly asleep.

The phone dragged her back to consciousness, feeling like the Wreck of the Hesperus. She hardly had the strength to lift the handset.

The quack down the earpiece was all too familiar. June.

'You all right, love?'

'Oh, yes . . . I've just got a migraine, June. I think I'll stay in bed today . . .'

'Anything you need?'

'No, nothing.'

'Shall I open up the shop for you? A closed antique-shop puts people off. I can look after both . . . it's all trade!'

'No, June. I need the quiet. I'll be all right if I have quiet. I know these migraines. I've got pills for them. I'll be all right tomorrow if I stay quiet today.'

'You musta had too much excitement yesterday. I've heard about the bed. Trev's here. He's rung Big Artie about it. It's all arranged . . . I'm dying to see it. We all are.'

'Not now, June . . .'

'All right, love. I'll leave you in peace then. Only I was worried about you. We saw your car parked outside, so we knew you weren't away buying. And Trev said to tell you that—'

'Not now, June, *please*!' She put the phone down quickly, before June could start again. It seemed a bit rude and ungrateful but . . . Lucy fell back into a black and dreamless sleep, with only a slight pang that Trev was next door, and today she wouldn't be seeing him.

June thanked Mr Patel for the use of his phone, and tried to give him ten pence, which he waved away. She crossed to her own shop, where Trev was keeping an eye on things, with one wooden chair tipped back against the wall, and his feet on another.

'She's all right, just a migraine. She's staying in bed today. Don't blame her.'

'Think we ought to cancel tonight?'

'She'll be all right by tonight. Our Harry gets migraines. They never last beyond five o'clock. He never misses the pub.'

'I'll be off then. Back to the grindstone.'

'Have you seen them Electricity buggers, digging up the road outside?' June peered back angrily through her doorway; up the street. 'I hope they don't start digging up the road outside *my* shop. They're a menace. Remember the last time? They took three weeks and nobody could park their car and trade just went *dead*. It was nearly the end of me.'

Trev took a good look at the big Electricity van, as he passed it. There was the usual scatter of orange plastic cones, and iron rods driven into the tarmac, with orange ribbons fluttering between them. One man, stripped to the waist, was making quite a long hole in the road, but it wasn't very deep.

'Going to take long?' Trev asked him.

'Only a little job,' said the man, resting both hands on his pick. 'Be gone by tomorrow.'

Trev studied him. He thought he had the wrong sort of

voice for a navvy; a bit too posh. And he wasn't very brown like they usually were, in spite of the good summer they were having. He wasn't very muscular, either; no passing lady motorists would waste time eyeing *him*.

Still, he thought, as he walked on, maybe the bloke was a student, working in his summer vac. He had the look of a student, with his long pale face and shock of dark hair, cut in a short version of an Afro. He had cocky bugger-you eyes . . .

Takes all sorts, Trev told himself, as he walked back to his pick-up. All part of life's rich tapestry. He must let June know the men weren't going to be there long . . . but it was hardly worth it. They'd be gone by tomorrow anyway . . .

There'd been other men inside the Electricity van; he'd heard them muttering. Drinking tea, he supposed. The British workman. No wonder the country was up the creek . . .

Above the shop sign 'Rachel Kingsmith Antiques' the two innocents slept peacefully on.

Chapter Seventeen

It was the cats who wakened her. Trampling on her face, demanding to be fed.

Half-past six. June would be long gone, thank heaven.

If anything, she felt even more shattered. But she staggered up, needing the loo badly. The cooling evening air refreshed her, as she went across the yard and back. She fed the cats and put the kettle on, and made another mug of tea for Daddy. But when she went upstairs with it, he was still fast asleep on his back, one arm over his eyes, as if to ward off the light, or a blow. The previous mug of tea, stone-cold, was still on the bedside table, untouched.

As if aware of her close study, he moaned a little and turned away from her. She tiptoed round the bed and studied him even closer. The long black whiskers . . . the new and deeper lines on his face, the pale transparency of his skin, threw her into a state of near-terror. *Could* people wear out as quickly as this? He looked so vulnerable asleep, like an ancient baby. He was only forty-five . . . Then a great flood of caring swept through her. She would guard him, she would nurse him back to what he had been, she would make up to him for everything that had happened to him . . .

It was then she heard the knocking on the shop door downstairs. A controlled tapping on the glass. She just knew it was June, come nosying. She went slowly and resentfully down, worrying how to repel June and all her concern.

175

Suppose Daddy wakened up, blundered downstairs, while she was getting rid of June? How could she explain his shabby gear, the holes in his socks? The lack of any car he might have driven up in?

So it was a relief to see the three men standing there, in their Electricity Board overalls. They could only want a look at her meter, at worst, and that was safely tucked away under the stairs. But she still hesitated.

The man in front, a silver-haired portly man, smiled at her, held up an identity card of some sort, with his photograph on it.

Reluctantly, she opened the door . . .

His elbow took her full in the stomach, sweeping her aside. She doubled up; the pain was agonizing, she couldn't speak, she couldn't breathe. All she knew was that the silver-haired man had hold of both her elbows from behind, and was bundling her into the dark depths of the shop, making her antiques rock and rattle. And that the other two men swept past and their feet made a soft thudding on the uncarpeted stairs.

The man let go of one of her elbows, and closed the shop door carefully and locked it. Then he said, 'Upstairs, girlie,' and bundled her upwards, twisting her arm so painfully she thought he was going to break it. Her legs were giving way under her, like rubber bands; the man had to thrust her upstairs by main force.

Daddy's bedroom door was wide open. Another man called softly, from inside, 'We've got him. In here!'

Daddy was sitting up in bed, staring about him in a fuddled way, as if he didn't know where he was.

'Nobody else here,' called the third man, from the bathroom. 'I'll check downstairs.' He came out with a long blue-black metal object in his hand. It didn't even look like a gun, with the long cylinder of the silencer.

Silence, as they all listened to him moving around downstairs, going out through the back door, coming back.

'Nobody else,' he called up the stairs softly. He came back into the room, putting the gun away inside his jacket. He had leather straps across his chest, to hold the gun in place. He was very thin, with close-cropped hair and a moustache; which made him look like a soldier.

'Not even *signs* of anybody else,' he repeated. 'Just the two of them.'

'Good,' said the silver-haired man, in a way that meant he was boss. 'OK. Get searching.'

He shoved Lucy on the bed, next to Daddy. She watched, as if from far away, as the two other men searched everywhere. They were incredibly quick, yet they disturbed nothing. Even when they lifted the rug from under her feet, to check the floorboards, they rearranged it back neatly, lifting her feet to do so. She just let them, watching in frozen fascination. She must be suffering from shock; she knew she couldn't speak. It would be too much effort.

The two men vanished into her own room. One of them called out, 'The stuff's here. Two packets of it. They've been opened.'

'Make sure there's nothing else.' Then the portly man turned to Lucy. 'Had a good look inside those packets, girlie, have you? The packets your daddy sent you?'

'*I* opened those packets,' said Daddy. 'When I got here. She knows nothing. She's only a child . . .'

The portly man gave a small unpleasant smile. 'In Northern Ireland, kids half her age are planting bombs . . .'

They all listened again in silence to the sounds. Drawers slamming open and shut; the side of the bath being unscrewed; later, the antiques downstairs being moved, then her kitchen stuff. A cat cried out. They must have trodden on its tail . . .

177

Finally, they came back and stood side by side, and said, 'Nothing else.'

'Sure? There'll be no clear-up team on this job, you know. Once we go, we go for good.'

'Nothing.'

'Right. Let's get them out, then. Check the street's clear. We're going to give you a little jab, girlie. Just to calm you down.'

Again, Daddy said desperately, 'She knows nothing. She's only a child . . .'

'You should've thought of that before you got her involved.'

The man with the Afro haircut, the one who didn't look like a soldier, got a small flat plastic case out of his overalls pocket, and opened it. There was a glint of steel and glass inside.

'This won't hurt, girlie,' said the plump man. 'No more than a little prick. Just like going to the dentist.' He had such a nasty smile. His eyes were the dull green of old wrinkled grapes.

She looked at Daddy. And knew he would just go on sitting there doing nothing. He'd given in.

What he didn't realize – what came to her then – was that these must be the men who killed Bettsy. Perhaps it had just been a little prick in the arm for Bettsy too. Perhaps he had gone, consenting, trusting.

Not her! Suddenly she was utterly alive, desperate with life. Anything to stop this being the last . . .

'I read them,' she said to the plump man. 'I read all the stuff.'

He just shrugged. A terrible little shrug that said it didn't matter. That it didn't matter what she said or did.

So she added, desperately, 'I photocopied them.'

'Photocopies?' The plump man suddenly gave her all his attention. So did the other two.

The Afro one said, 'There weren't any extra copies in the envelopes. Just one of each. I checked.'

The soldier one added quickly, 'There weren't no photocopies anywhere else.'

'You *sure*?'

'Nowhere. It's not a big house.'

'Undersides of drawers? Backs of cupboards?'

'I tell you I looked; everywhere.'

The plump man switched his eyes back to Lucy.

'Pull the other leg, girlie. It's got bells on it.' But was there just a flicker of doubt . . . ?

'I posted them,' said Lucy, staring at him very hard.

'Where to?'

'The *New York Herald Tribune*. The *Washington Post. Figaro* . . .'

'And what would their *addresses* be?'

Even now triumph was sweet. She still had the photographic memory that had always helped her so much in exams. She reeled off the addresses perfectly, one after the other.

'Jesus H. Christ,' said Afro, softly.

The plump man stared at Lucy a long long time. Then he said, 'She's just playing for time. She's making it up. Let's get going.'

And they all began to move again.

Until there was the sound of a car outside on the road that didn't go past; that pulled up with a squeak of handbrake and stopped its engine.

The soldier had flattened himself to the window-side. Now he squinted out, and mouthed, near-silently, 'Red Escort. F132 GNE. Man and a woman. Woman's got long red hair. They're getting out.'

179

Lucy's heart leapt. The Escort was Ken's. The girl sounded like Jessie. Were they coming to see her?

The plump man grabbed her from behind, twisting her arm, putting a hand across her mouth. The soldier had got out his gun again, and was pointing it straight at Daddy's face.

Ken's voice came floating up through the partly open window.

'I hope the four of us can get it upstairs. That stair's bloody narrow . . .'

Jessie said, 'I can't wait to see it. Trev made it sound marvellous.'

They were talking about Lucy's bed.

Someone tapped quietly on the shop door.

Nobody in the room moved.

Somebody knocked again, harder.

'Wonder where she's got to?' said Ken. 'She can't be far. Her car's here.'

'Maybe she can't hear you. Maybe she's got the radio on.'

A deeper silence. Lucy thought the plump man holding her didn't even breathe.

'Can't hear any radio,' said Ken. 'She's not got one of those Walkmans, has she?'

'I can't imagine Rachel with a Walkman. Maybe she's nipped down to the shop.'

'We're a bit early. Fancy a drink? Pub's only fifty yards.'

'Don't mind if I do.'

Their footsteps faded away. Lucy's heart sank. Again, the three men in the room came to life. Afro began fiddling with the syringe he took from the case.

Then Lucy heard Jessie call out, 'Here's Trev coming now. He'll know what's happened.'

Their footsteps came back. Trev's heavy engine cut out, under the window.

The men froze again; but they were mouthing to each

other, in tones that didn't carry more than two yards. She could tell they'd worked together for a long time; they didn't waste words.

'Check the back.'

Afro slid away silently, then slid back.

'Back gate's locked.'

'Break it.'

'Big padlock.'

'Break it.'

Afro slid away again, like a ghost.

Trev's voice outside; worried. 'She should be here. She was lying down. Said she had a migraine. Didn't open the shop today. I hope she's all right.'

There came a harder knocking still. Then Trev said, 'I'll go round the back and check. Maybe there's a window I can get open.'

'She's got window-bars.'

'Not upstairs. Maybe I can get up on the kitchen roof . . .'

There was the sound of his running, worried footsteps.

Afro slid back into the room *very* swiftly, but still silently. He shrugged; waited for more orders. But, for the first time, the plump man seemed to have difficulty in thinking of any.

There was the sound of another approaching engine; heavier; a diesel.

'Here's Big Artie,' said Jessie. 'He's brought his lad, thank God. You should manage the bed now.'

'What's up?' asked Big Artie, getting out. 'Don't bloody tell me she's not in. Getting that bed aboard nearly killed Jack an' me. I don't want to do it again. I'd have to charge her double, for two journeys.'

'Trev thinks she's home,' said Jessie. 'Her car's here. She's just not answering the door. Trev thinks she's poorly. She had a migraine this morning.'

Lucy felt the plump man's hands tense up. The more people that were arriving, the more tense he was getting.

'She might be really ill,' said Big Artie. 'She mighta fallen downstairs or anything. Where's Trev?'

'Round the back. Trying to get in the top window.'

'Mebbe we'll have to break the door down,' said Big Artie. There was the sound of him rattling the door viciously. 'I don't think this lock's up to much.'

'Don't do that,' said Jessie. 'I think June's got a spare key. I'll go and ring her. She can be down here in five minutes.'

'We can ring from Patel's,' said Ken. 'He's open till ten. I'll come with you. I need some fags.'

'And I could do wi' a can o' lager,' said the near-mute lad of Artie's.

Their footsteps started away.

'Only one left,' mouthed the soldier, raising his black eyebrows in a question mark.

The plump man nodded.

Swiftly, silently, the soldier squeezed past and vanished downstairs, gun again in his hand. At the same time the plump man jerked Lucy forward, to follow him. His hand was still across her mouth, hard. His other hand still held her arm twisted cruelly up her back. Behind, she heard Daddy give a gasp of pain, as he too was jerked to his feet.

Going downstairs was excruciating; she felt her arm was being pulled off; the pain made her gasp for breath.

But from the bottom of the stair, she saw it all. Big Artie standing with his back to the shop door, outside, rocking his massive frame back and forwards on his heels in frustration. Waiting impatiently for the others to come back. All innocent and trusting.

And she saw the soldier, the heavy gun reversed in his right hand now, reaching for the lock. He would hit Artie

from behind; Artie would never know what had hit him . . .
The lock turned silently; the door opened silently; a slight
evening breeze blew in. Still Artie did not turn; he was
whistling mournfully between his teeth; his boots grinding
gently in the road-grit lying on the footpath.

The plump man felt Lucy tense up; his fingers fastened
hard across her mouth; his other hand began to twist her
arm even tighter.

It was now or never.

She drew back her lips and bit on those fingers. With all
the strength in her jaw. Her teeth closed on only one; but it
split like a piece of warm fruit and there was a sweet taste of
blood in her mouth. And then the fingers were gone, as,
behind her, the plump man gasped, in agony.

She filled her lungs with one long gulp, and screamed.

The heave on her arm brought her, crunching and gasping, to her knees. But she heard a thud, and then she heard
Big Artie curse, very horribly, and knew the soldier had hit
him and failed to knock him out.

She was dragged to her feet again. And saw Big Artie was
indeed neither down nor out. He had backed away to the
open door of his truck; he was rubbing his shoulder, as if it
hurt. As she watched, he reached behind him and pulled
something long from the floor of the van. It looked like a
big iron tyre-lever . . .

And from across the road, footsteps, running.

Mr Patel called out, 'What is happening? What is
happening?'

And then they were all grouped round Big Artie; Mr
Patel, Ken, Jessie, Artie's lad all gaping incomprehendingly
at . . .

The long blue-black gun in the soldier's hand. With the
muzzle pointing at them now; swinging from side to side, to
include them all.

183

Then Trev's voice from the side, calling, 'I can't get that window open; it's rusted solid.' Then, 'What the . . .?'

The swinging muzzle of the gun included Trev too. Shocked, open-mouthed, helpless, like the rest of them. Five utterly helpless people . . .

Lucy felt the agonizing pressure from behind again. Forcing her out of the shop door, up the street. Towards a big Electricity Board van. Sounds of Daddy being forced along behind her.

The plump man reached round and opened the van's rear door, and thrust her in on her face. Then climbed over her and dragged her along the steel floor. Behind, she heard Daddy gasp in pain again. The door was slammed shut and locked. Feet trampled roughly over her. The van engine roared into life.

The front passenger door of the van opened and shut, and she could hear the soldier panting.

Then the van was away, at a speed that sent her rolling across into a pile of hard objects.

'Get back here!' ordered the plump man.

Lucy saw the soldier's trainers come over the back of the seat, missing her face by inches. Watched him grope his way, hand over hand, down the bucketing van. Then the soldier called, 'Shit, they're following. Big pick-up.'

Trev.

'They've got three aerials on the pick-up,' said the soldier, very calmly. 'That means CB radio. They could raise the whole bloody country.'

'Take them out,' said the plump man. 'Get their radiator if you can.'

There was the sound of two or three sharp blows and a tinkle of glass as the rear-windows of the van shattered outwards. Craning her neck, Lucy watched the soldier brace himself, legs stretched far apart, both arms out through a broken window. He looked very expert . . .

He was going to shoot Trev.

'Ease up, Barry,' said the plump man to the driver. 'Let them get a bit closer.'

The van slowed. But the soldier said, 'They've eased up too. Just following. That big bloke wasn't born yesterday.'

'He was in Two Para,' said Lucy, full of spite.

The plump man raised a foot and kicked her in the ribs, very painfully. 'Shut up, girlie!'

The gun exploded once, deafening in the narrow space. Then again. Oh, Trev, Trev . . .

'Bloody useless,' said the soldier in disgust. 'Find me a straight bit of road.'

'There aren't any straight bits on this road,' said Barry.

'Clap your anchors on,' said the plump man. 'Then reverse up to them, before they can turn.'

The van's brakes squealed; the gears whined in reverse. The van began to roll backwards . . .

'Oh, *nice*,' said the soldier. His gun exploded twice again. Then he said, 'Oh, shit.'

'What?'

'He put his lights on. Quartz-halogens. I can't see a bloody thing. And *he's* reversing.'

'Get to a big town, Barry. We can lose them . . .' The plump man's voice was definitely not quite so calm as it had been.

They bucketed forward again. After a while, the one called Barry said, 'Bloody Huddersfield, twenty.' In utter disgust. And she felt the van swerve round a steep turn.

It was a strange endless time that followed. She managed to crawl right into the corner, behind the passenger seat, where she could sit upright without provoking the plump man's kicks. The interior of the van was a shambolic mess. Newspapers all over the floor, everything from the *Mirror* to *The Times*, which the men must have read during their vigil outside the shop. Half-eaten sandwiches trampled flat among them. In the corner, an Elsan chemical loo seemed to have come adrift from its moorings with all the swerving they'd done at speed. Dark liquid leaked from it; the smell was indescribable.

Every so often, the soldier braced himself and fired his gun again, with a weary boredom in which there was little hope. But Lucy held her breath till it hurt, in the gap between the explosion and the short sharp burst of obscenity which meant he'd missed again. Sometimes the light of Trev's quartz-halogen lamps poured in through the broken back windows of the van like a brilliant yellow flood, making the soldier curse and shield his eyes. The yellow flood grew stronger and stronger, and she realized the daylight was waning. The clouds were heavy; it would be dark early tonight . . .

And all the time, on the little moorland road, other cars kept passing them, in both directions, with a little whoom and shudder, quite innocent to what was going on.

'He mustn't have had any luck with his CB radio,' said the soldier at last.

'Who'd take any notice of him?' said the plump man. 'Who'd believe him? They'll reckon he's a hoaxer.'

Daddy just lay and listened. Sometimes he tried to smile at her; but the smile didn't work. If Daddy tried to say anything, the plump man kicked him. Soon it grew so dark in the van, she couldn't even see Daddy's expression. Her only hope was in the brilliant quartz-halogen beam that from time to time lit up every weld in the roof of the van.

'We're coming down into Huddersfield,' said the driver.

186

'They'll *have* to close in now,' said the plump man. 'Or lose us. Then you can settle them.'

Through the rear windows, Lucy could see orange street-lamps passing in succession.

'They're closing up,' said the solider, grim satisfaction in his voice. He leaned forward and took aim carefully.

'Shit,' said the driver. 'Traffic lights. Against us.'

'Jump them!'

'Can't. There's big stuff crossing.' The brakes went on with a squeal. Looking over her shoulder, Lucy could see the enormous crawling bulk of an approaching juggernaut, crossing their front.

And then, from behind, an even greater squealing of brakes. The light of Trev's quartz-halogens on the roof of the van grew blinding, incandescent. And then there was an impact that drove the breath out of Lucy's lungs. The soldier seemed to fly through the air over her head. There was a crash of glass as the windscreen went. And a tremendous grinding from the front, dragging them sideways. The smell of petrol . . .

She must get out; she must get Daddy out.

She managed to get to her feet, by clawing up the back of the passenger seat. The feet of the soldier hung down the dashboard; the rest of his body was through the wind-screen, lying on the bonnet of the van, motionless. The man Barry was slumped over the wheel, groaning softly to himself. Of the plump man there was no sign. But the passenger door was crumpled and wide open; cool evening air blew in.

She climbed over the seat towards it. Turned to drag Daddy after her. He was still conscious, crawling, trying to help. Together they fell through the door on to the ground. Her back hurt so much she didn't try to move again; just stared around from ground level.

187

The great wheels of the now-stationary juggernaut they'd crashed into. A great blue cliff with the lettering CHRISTIAN SALVESON on it. Beyond, a smashed traffic-light, leaning at an angle but still, weirdly, working. Red, amber, green . . .

Against its switching colours, two men were standing. The plump man, swaying like a drunk. With his left hand he held a hanky to his face, half-white, half-red with blood.

Facing him, the towering bulk of Big Artie, with his iron tyre-lever still in his hand. Shouting, 'I'll kill ya! I'll damn well kill ya!'

But he didn't move, and neither did Trev, standing white-faced behind him. Because there was a pistol in the plump man's hand now. It wavered and drooped, but it still pointed at Big Artie.

And beyond the smashed traffic-light, murmuring, straining forward and then straining back, a crowd was gathering, more every minute; a sea of blurred faces, staring.

And Big Artie watched the gun waver, waiting his chance with an eagerness that made Lucy shudder.

'He's got a gun,' murmured the crowd. 'He's got a gun. Get the police.' Then, 'Listen! The police are coming, the police are coming, the police are coming.'

And then the sound of police-car sirens.

The man Barry staggered from the van, his face a mask of drying blood. He tugged urgently at the plump man's sleeve. But the plump man wouldn't listen. His little gun swung, from the figure of Big Artie, edging forward by inches, to the growing crowd.

'Get back!' he shouted. 'Get back!'

Lucy could almost pity him; he moved this way and that, like a crippled dying insect.

Now there were policemen's caps, bobbing among the crowd, shouting orders, trying to move them back. Slowly the crowd dissolved away, leaving only the policemen watching, from the cover of the crashed van and shop doorways. Talking softly into their radios.

While the plump man, in some world of his own in which only the menacing waiting figure of Big Artie was real, continued to sway and wave his drooping gun.

It seemed to go on for ever, until a sharp electronic voice said, 'Armed police. Drop your gun.'

It seemed to penetrate the plump man's fuddled mind. The gun drooped slowly in his pudgy fingers, till it fell, with a tiny rattle, on the road. Then there was a rush of policemen, as he too fell on his face, dragging down the man Barry with him.

A policeman in a short bulky black jacket was bending over Lucy.

'Are you all right, miss?'

'Help my father. I think he's hurt. And there's another man in the van . . .'

'I'm afraid *he's* dead, miss.'

Lucy sat across the desk from a huge policeman. His shirt was so white it was dazzling; his tunic glittered with so many badges of rank it was impossible to tell what rank he really was. His face was not particularly kind, though he was trying hard to make it so. But his voice was sharp with suppressed rage as he said, 'I would be grateful if *somebody* could tell me what's been going on in my city. One man dead, three in hospital, one gibbering about the needs of national security and two more gibbering about kidnapping . . . You seem to be the only one who's in their right mind. Could you please start again, with your name and address?'

Lucy's mind wavered feebly. Should she be Lucy Smith or Rachel Kingsmith? She couldn't make her mind up; it was beyond her. And there was a handsome policewoman waiting in the corner to record every word she said. After a long pause, and many hesitations, she decided to tell the truth.

'Lucy Rachel King Smith, daughter of William Hargreaves Smith . . .'

The policeman gave a slight start; he recognized the names all right. He leaned forward with keen interest.

And then the phone rang on his desk. He snatched it up as if he would have liked to eat it whole, and the person on the far end with it, and roared, 'Yes?'

After quite a short while he said, outraged, 'Secret service? They crash their van at a main city intersection, when the streets are full of people out for the evening! They threaten my policemen with a gun, in front of hundreds of onlookers! And you say they're supposed to be the *secret* service? They're about as secret as the Eurovision Song Contest. Listen, I've got ten reporters in the lobby now, clamouring to know if this is Chicago. What am I supposed to tell *them*?'

More agitated quacking from the phone, which Lucy couldn't quite make out. Then the policeman said, 'What's this number you want me to ring?' He wrote a number down, then rang off and dialled it, and when it answered roared, 'Who the hell is this I'm supposed to be talking to?'

His face changed subtly as he listened. But his voice was still fairly savage as he said, 'You mean these bloody criminal lunatics are *yours*?'

A little later, still cooling down, he said, 'I can't do that. I've got a young girl here, in a state of shock. There are allegations she's been kidnapped. At gunpoint. She looks scared out of her wits. No, I don't care what her father's done. Her father's in hospital, having a check-up. I'm going to have her hospitalized too, when she's finished talking to me. I'm not taking any chances with this one. I'm playing it by the book.'

The phone quacked on, with increasing agitation.

'Look,' said the policeman, 'I don't care how big this is. I'll talk to the Home Secretary. I'll talk to the bloody Prime Minister if you like. But I'm not brushing this under the carpet like some Cabinet minister with a drunk-driving ticket. Not that I'd do that either, mind. And I'm not letting anybody go, till I know what's going on. I'll nick the lot of them and hold them till morning, and that's as far as I'm going . . .'

The phone grew hysterical.

'Look, it's too late to hush it up. The West Yorkshire police are involved too – complaint of kidnapping made by a respectable shopkeeper and about ten antique-dealers. How do you suggest I shut *them* up? Do you suggest that I arrest them too? And all the mates they've already told about it? On what charge? Seeing what they shouldn't have done?'

Quack, quack, quack.

'Look, mate, this cat's out of the bag good and proper, and nothing on earth is going to get it back in. I'm not risking my pension pulling your chestnuts out of the fire. We happen to have two very stroppy opposition MPs in this city, just waiting to nail the police if we blink the wrong eyelash . . . No doubt the Home Secretary will know their names. And their reputations . . .'

The quacking changed to a wail.

'Look, mate, we're just ordinary coppers here. We don't play politics. I'm getting to the bottom of this. I'm probably the last to know – I expect it's all over my canteen already . . .'

Wail. The policeman's voice gathered, if anything, an

191

extra viciousness. 'I'm not having what happened to John Stalker happening to me. You buggered up his career, but you're not buggering up mine . . . We've not forgotten John Stalker, up here.'

Vaguely, Lucy remembered the John Stalker business. When she was little he'd been Deputy Chief Constable of Manchester or something, sent to investigate the RUC's alleged shoot-to-kill policy. He'd asked too many questions, been suspended from duty on a trumped-up charge, been cleared, then resigned at a very young age, career ruined . . .

There was obviously a deep rift between the Government and the police, which she'd never have dreamt was there. Oh, the world was such a strange odd place; you could almost die of the strangeness and oddness . . .

The policeman banged down the phone, pulled an awful grimace and said to Lucy, 'C'mon, young lady. Let's hear *all* about it.'

Blessing his angry honest face, she laid aside all doubts and told everything she knew.

Chapter Eighteen

She felt more and more unreal; tucked up in a hospital bed like a baby, while they fussed over her. Not even allowed a dressing-gown or an arm-chair, just this wretched shroud-like thing that did up down the back where she couldn't properly reach. In a room by herself; door guarded by a young policeman tipped back on a tubular chair in the corridor, reading a paperback with a near-naked blonde firing a sub-machine-gun its greasy wrinkled cover. Snatches of voices echoed up the corridor; nurses' voices, police-men's voices, once Trev's and Artie's, raised in protest. But she couldn't make out what they were saying; what was going on.

The big policeman last night, having questioned her over and over again till one in the morning, and got her to sign a very long statement, had suddenly turned solicitous for her health and summoned an ambulance. She had ridden across the deserted city facing an ambulance man and a policeman who eyed and spoke to her at short regular intervals, as if she was something both precious and poten-tially explosive.

Since then she had been wheeled out all over the endless hospital corridors, for an ECG and an EEG and many x-rays. She had given nurses samples of everything she had to give and been gone over with a fine-tooth comb by two young doctors, one male, one female. They poked her often and painfully; looked at each other inscrutably every time she yelled. They had shone lights in her eyes and made her wriggle her toes and then gone off tutting at each other, heads close together. She had finally fallen asleep and been instantly wakened with a cup of tea, which she drank eagerly, then a breakfast that she could not face. In the few moments of privacy allowed her, she had eased up her shroud and seen that she had the most spectacular bruises in places she hadn't dreamt you could have bruises.

She felt like asserting her rights; but somehow she knew she had no rights. Not even the right to her shroud, which people undid without asking her permission.

Above all, everyone was seething with excitement, their eyes shining with questions they dared not ask. Everyone kept peering out of the windows at the crowd of reporters and photographers who were gathered at the hospital gate. And two TV outside-broadcast vans. She felt halfway between a murderess and a pop-star.

And whenever she asked about Daddy, people just said he was 'comfortable' . . .

Finally, Daddy himself had come in. He limped with the aid of a stick, but he was freshly shaved and wearing a very expensive-looking dressing-gown, and his eyes gleamed with excitement. This was a different Daddy. The lost weary wanderer of the motorways, with terrible holes in his socks, was gone. Daddy was back in the realm of ideas, statements and discussions where he truly belonged. Still, he leant over to kiss her, but was awkward with the stick and over-balanced on top of her; and they both said 'Ow' then laughed and held each other close; closer than they'd held each other since Mummy died, and it was wonderful, the smell of him, the warmth of him through the dressing-gown.

But there were other men, behind him, watching; and all too soon he broke away and went business-like and brisk.

'Lucy, you remember Mr Coates, my solicitor? Well now

he's your solicitor too. He'll be acting for you, during your trial.'

'Trial?' she faltered.

But Mr Coates, vaguely remembered from the reading of Mummy's will, was holding out his hand to her. He had a shining bald head, but otherwise looked very young and brown and fit. He gave her a sympathetic smile and said, 'We hope to get you out on bail; within a few days. Not much hope of that for your father, I'm afraid.'

'Not to worry,' said Daddy. 'Wait till you hear who we've got as our barrister. Neill Bowden, MP, QC, the Shadow Home Secretary! He's cutting short his holiday in the South of France and flying up tonight. A real big gun, Lucy, and with us all the way. All the Opposition are.'

She gasped. She'd seen Neill Bowden on the telly, with his snub nose and wavy hair and beautiful suits, and the terribly rude things he said about the Government. Suddenly she felt a touch of hope. Which was as well, for the next moment a very different sort of man stepped forward. A thin small man whose cold blue eyes didn't like her at all. The room seemed to go suddenly freezing.

'And this,' said Daddy, in a very different sort of voice, 'is Chief Inspector Lillie of Special Branch. He's come to charge and caution you, Lucy. Just listen and don't say anything to him at all.' Daddy reached across from the chair someone had fetched him and held both her hands very tight in his. While the Chief Inspector took a sheaf of papers out of his briefcase and began to read from them.

'Lucy Rachel King Smith, I hereby charge you . . .' He went on and on, and she only heard occasional words like 'conspiracy' and 'theft of documents' and 'breach of national security' over and over. Then he said, 'You need not say anything now, but anything you do say will be taken down and may be given in evidence.'

195

Then he turned on his heel and walked away.

This isn't happening, thought Lucy. This just isn't happening.

But Mr Coates smiled grimly at his retreating back and said, 'Poor sod. He doesn't know which side of the fence to jump down on. One wrong step and he could be up in court himself next week. Charged with God knows what.'

Daddy's grip on her hands tightened. 'Don't look so worried, kitten. It's going to be all right. Your jiffy-bags got through. People believed them. The *Washington Post* ran the stuff yesterday – it's all over America. And *Figaro* and *Il Tempo* published this morning. By tonight, the whole world will be howling for this Government's blood. Oh, they'll fight, Lucy, fight and cheat and lie all the way to stay in power. But they haven't a prayer. They'll be dragged down screaming by inches. Just like Nixon after Watergate. Once the truth *starts* coming out, there's no stopping it . . .'

'Just for whales?' stammered Lucy. It seemed a terrible upheaval to make, just about whales.

'Whales aren't the half of it. Whales aren't the tenth of it. But the whales put me on to it. Why the whale-stocks weren't recovering . . . Why whales are dying. And why the Government was trying to cover up the fact.'

'*Why?*'

'The dumping of toxic waste, Lucy. In mid-ocean. Mercury in the Marianas Trench. Cadmium in the mid-Atlantic Trench. The oceans are becoming toxic cess-pits, Lucy.'

She shuddered. The oceans had always seemed the last free clean space . . .

'And on land too, Lucy. Africa, South America. Natives who don't know any better are building huts out of drums of radioactive waste. Little kids are paddling in rivers full of arsenic compounds. It's called toxic imperialism, Lucy. And it's British firms who are doing it. Titra Export, Braithwaite

Shipping and Haulage, Eurokem. Firms nobody's heard about till now – except the Government who was covering up for them, hiding them, giving them export licences and no questions asked . . . But, by God, the world'll hear about them now. They used to call Britain the Workshop of the World. Now we've become the Dustbin of the World. But not in our own back yard . . . let the Third World die . . . it can't feed itself anyway. So what's it matter?'

'But the foreign factories . . . the new ones they're building?'

'Payment for services rendered. Those countries create more toxic waste than anybody . . . so they show their gratitude.'

Lucy's head spun.

Daddy said, 'Governments are like wild beasts, Lucy. They will kill to stay alive.'

'I know,' she said. 'I think . . . they murdered Mr Betts.'

After that, it was Daddy and Mr Coates who did the listening.

Now it was all over. They had gone.

And the doctors and nurses had finished with her; there was nothing wrong with her, save bruises.

Two WPCs came in. 'Fetch her clothes,' said the taller one to the nurse.

They watched her dress; she did not dare to look at them. They made impatient noises while she put up her chignon; but she made them wait. If she was going to prison, she would go in style.

The smaller one looked out of the window. 'More all the time,' she said. 'There's another telly van now.'

'I don't want a blanket tossed over me,' said Lucy. 'It'll ruin my hair.'

The two WPCs said nothing.

She walked down the corridor in front of them. In a slow dignified way, keeping her head up. As Mummy would have done.

At the end of the corridor, Trev came blundering out of a side ward, pushing between two policemen. He had a bandage round his head. With his spectacles, it made him look a bit like a studious pirate.

'We had to crash into you,' he said. 'It was the only way of stopping them. Big Artie said it would be all right. We were doing under thirty. I suppose we overdid it.'

'That man's . . . dead,' said Lucy.

Trev winced, and looked utterly lost. Then he clenched his jaw with an effort and said, 'He was trying to kill us. He put two bullets into my windscreen. Only the Perspex saved us. I knew it would come in handy some day.'

But he didn't look as brave as his words. He looked like a small boy who had got into a fight, then realized he had bitten off far more than he could possibly chew. It must be terrible, to see a man dead, and know you'd killed him.

'Thanks,' she said, as warmly as she could manage. 'Thanks for saving my life.'

'All part of life's rich tapestry, I suppose.' But his grin was a ghost of its former self. Even if the law found him not guilty of anything, she knew he was going to pay a terrible price inside himself for what he'd done.

They were all going to pay a terrible price; win or lose.

The two WPCs were pushing at her elbows from behind, and she had to start walking again.

'They're letting me and Artie out on bail,' Trev yelled after her. 'We'll keep the shop going for you. Feed the cats. Till you get back . . .'

'I'll get you clocks, love,' yelled Big Artie from behind him. 'Plenty o' clocks. An' chairs . . . good chairs!'

And suddenly, amidst all the terrible prices that were going to be paid, it was all right. At the end of it all, the shop and the cats would be waiting. The thing she had made for herself. And June and Ken and Flora and all of them.

Tears came to her eyes, but she held her head *up*.

'Thanks,' she shouted back, in a half-strangled voice.

Then Lucy Rachel King Smith walked on to her fate.

About the Author

ROBERT WESTALL was a renowned author of books for adults and young adults and is the recipient of two Carnegie Medals, the Guardian Award, and a Smarties Prize in his native England.

This is Robert Westall's sixth book for Scholastic Hardcover. His previous works include: *In Camera and Other Stories, Yaxley's Cat, The Promise, Blitzcat,* and *Ghost Abbey.*

LAKE ZURICH MIDDLE SCHOOL
NORTH CAMPUS
LAKE ZURICH, ILLINOIS 60047

LAKE ZURICH MIDDLE SCHOOL
NORTH CAMPUS
LAKE ZURICH, ILLINOIS 60047